The Challenge of the Darrn

Patrick S. Tremblay

ISBN-13: 978-0-9883135-1-4

DEDICATION

This book is for my family.

CONTENTS

ACKNOWLEDGMENTS

For my wife Elizabeth, and my children Kaitlyn, Hayden, and Sophia whose enthusiasm for my stories on long trips gave me the encouragement to finish this particular book. Thanks to Amanda Tremblay, my little sister and writing soundboard. Our childhood gave me inspiration for certain scenes in this book. Thanks to my oldest sister, Cheryl Sitton for introducing me to reading. Thanks to my brothers, Steve, Gregory, and Karl Tremblay for showing me how to work hard for everything and never quit. And for my mother, Marie Tremblay-Continelli, thank you for the phone calls, funny stories, and the many reminders to finish what I start.

Special thanks to my friend Kendra Geiger, for painstakingly editing this book, so that everyone can enjoy this Darrn world.

1. THE PREMONITION

Montserrat, the surviving heir to the Darr Empire, awoke drenched with sweat and anxiety. He rolled onto his back and looked up toward the morning sky. As he focused on the first rays of light through his sensor shield, he took in a long breath and sighed heavily. The five moons of the Manta sector were vanishing into the new day without a trace. By the time he'd risen, robed, and finished his breakfast, he watched as the last moon sparkled before the brilliant day swallowed its radiance.

Walking out of his chamber, he strolled over to the heavily curtained opening to his balconied observatory. Montserrat noticed how the morning dew shone on the backs of the courtyard's many Argus—a giant bird resembling an earth species called the peacock—made their way around the floating city's limestone palace steps. The Argus' green and blue plumage was magnificent as they strutted through their morning routine. He could also detect the shimmer of the palace guards, a species called the Trans, known to be extremely volatile warriors in battle and unmatched in the art of defense, and who were semi-transparent to the naked eye. One floated by the port of the young heir's chamber and looked at him briefly revealing its gem-like eyes that flashed like faceted aquamarine. Without this trademark, the imperial guards were undetectable. Today their eyes beamed less as a sign of warning; something was causing alarm throughout the palace because the guards' eyes had changed to light blue. Just yesterday, they were darker.

"Could it have something to do with the arrival of the Imperial Master of the Guard, Minnion, on his sky-yacht, or maybe it was something else more terrible?" the prince asked himself.

Genetically half-Darrn and half-human, Minnion, was the largest and most fierce warrior in the empire. Minnion, one of the few living abominations of this breed, was merciless in tactics on the battlefield. He had only one equal, The Great Valnass.

Minnion and The Great Valnass were schooled from infancy as trustees to the throne and were devoted supporters of the Emperor. He and The Great Valnass, the reigning champion of the Cyclo arena, were best friends until the last days of Valnass' life.

Montserrat shuddered and his heart pounded as he turned toward his private exit. Now dressed in his battle gear for his morning training, his entourage of valets exited the room as quickly and quietly as they had appeared. Though now alone, Montserrat couldn't get his heart rate to slow down; something was causing him to be on guard. With a gesture of his finger, a door swished open as his sword hand returned to the hilt attached to the shield belt. Just as he was leaving his room for his arms lesson, he heard something and turned, and immediately felt the heat before he saw it! A Darrn, eight-feet tall with horrific breath and rotting teeth, spat molten saliva on the prince before he could defend himself and ripped the young man's face off with one jerk of its enormous fangs.

Montserrat, startled awake, jumped out of bed, gasped for breath and started shaking with immense fear. When he realized he was still alone and apparently safe in his apartment, he found his bearing. He sighed with such relief that he began to laugh. "I need to relax," he muttered to himself as he walked into his bathroom. Stepping into his shower, Montserrat thought of his birth-world, Darr, his mother the Queen, and the Emperor, the man he knew as his father.

"Will I ever return to Darr?" the young prince asked himself.

Currently, Montserrat was in exile on Earth, the third planet from the smallest star that his father's vast empire ruled. He chose this planet because it was so uncharted and insignificant that nothing could trace him there. He didn't have any deep feelings for this small galaxy in this universe, and he liked its inhabitants even less. They were constantly in planetary civil war: killing each other and destroying their small planet, a beautiful oasis for the most mundane reasons. On Darr it was mostly peaceful; only the beasts called the Darrn, who lived on the neighboring planet, caused any problems. He should not be fearful here on Earth, yet he was fully conscious that the bad feeling he'd been awakened by was growing stronger.

After collecting himself, Montserrat went on his way to the local university three blocks from his home. There he could blend in as a student and study the history and technology of this planet. "If only these humans could comprehend what resources this planet holds for them! If they just knew that the most powerful weapon in the universe was used as common jewelry and decoration. It's right in front of them, and they can't see past the most adolescent truths such as the theory of relativity and quantum physics! The flowers and foliage alone are worth an Emperor's ransom!" thought Montserrat as he entered through the glass doors of the institute's library. Rubbing his tight shoulders, Montserrat tried but still couldn't release the tension he sensed. Unfortunately, his questions of uncertainty were suddenly answered as the ceiling of the school library was ripped off like the top of a can. A Darrn hovered over the entrance it had just made for itself. Chaos broke out in a screaming frenzy, and every human ran to the nearest door to escape the sight. Immediately, Montserrat defensively executed a protective shield from his belt in hopes to save what knowledge these poor humans had acquired. This wouldn't last long because his shield-belt was engineered for one person. The Darrn began atomizing anything that moved but anyone or anything under the shield was now safe. The Darrn, with its fanged mouth and sinister bloodshot eyes, stared with hatred and mocked Montserrat. The prince had forgotten how hideous these beasts were and was appalled to hear his name spoken by one of these disgusting creatures.

"Prince Montserrat, you will return with me at once to face the trial of the Darrn," spat the beast.

At his name being spoken, Montserrat's shape began to transform into his true proportion. It could not be contained any longer without jeopardizing his defense against the Darrn. As a human, the prince stood six feet tall and weighed 220 pounds. This was a normal scale for humans, but off scale to the size of his true anatomy. On Darr, Montserrat was 7'8" and weighed a muscular 336 pounds. The Darrn shot a holding beam at Montserrat but missed, as the Prince spun around and raised his now outstretched hand. Montserrat returned the assault with five energy beams from his hand at the hideous intruder. The beams knocked the creature back, and it crashed into the side of the Building of Medicine. A woman in her late forties ran out of the building to see what the clamor was about when she saw the creature as it was rising from its collision. The Darrn grabbed the human by the head and tore it off in one sweeping blur. Her body continued to walk headless until it walked into a railing and crumbled to the floor. The creature squeezed the head until it oozed through its clawed hand; then it began to lick its hand as if it was an animal giving itself a bath. It was revolting, and only made Montserrat more infuriated. In a matter of seconds, he shot another energy beam at the Darrn, and it severed off the creatures arm at the shoulder.

The Darrn raged in pain and howled, "You will pay for your actions, fool!"

The beast flew into a high arc and dove at the Prince. With its one clawed arm and fangs bared, it roared toward its prey, intending to rip the young prince apart. Montserrat thought vehemently, "This can go on no longer!" With his arms generating an energy ball, Montserrat lowered his head in a sinister gaze and shot his weapon at the approaching beast. The energy blast tore away at the Darrn's thick, scaly torso until its chest blew apart. A look of revengeful hunger ran across his face as Montserrat catapulted enough blasts into the Darrn that by the time the carcass dropped to the floor, it was nothing but a flaming lump of cinder.

Heaving with massive breaths of air and his face revealing his total desire for destruction, Montserrat glared around at his surroundings and was frightened to see the many stunned bystanders. Instantly, he was aware of the blood boiling within his soul and could not quell his feelings to annihilate whatever was around him. Turning, he ran from the devastation, leaving his destructive feelings and his hope of new found peace behind.

As Montserrat came out of his fury, it was getting dark; he had returned to his apartment without knowing how he had made it back. Once alone, memories of Darr began to flood his thoughts. When Montserrat was on his home-world he had contended in the royal arena by law because of his heritage. With the overwhelming pressure of his inherited duties, a young Montserrat had fled from his life on Darr to abandon his inevitable involvement with defending the throne. Since he was hidden on earth up until now, he had been protected from the Call-of-Power challenge. Now with Montserrat coming of age, he would be hunted down until he returned to the Cathedral of Cyclo to defend his race from the Darrn, who were trying to take control of the nobility of Darr.

He gathered his possessions, stole away into the night and to made his way to his starship he had camouflaged in a boarded cave in the neighboring woods. Approaching the cave's mouth, he pulled out his receiver to disengage his cloaking device, but to his astonishment the ship had been exposed and brutally ransacked. Nothing was salvageable, and he could still smell the lingering foul stench of the Darrn. A small glow of red light pulsated in a pile of rubble and caught Montserrat's attention; upon approaching the red glow, he destroyed the device with one crushing blow of his boot. The Darrn had left behind an activated Hunter which was transmitting a locating beacon for other Darrn squads to intercept. Montserrat realized at once the Darrn he had fought at the University had stumbled across the faint signal from his ship, but he couldn't understand how the beast had found its precise location. Desperate he now rummaged to find his birthstone—the only object he'd left onboard which revealed his true lineage. This birthstone glowed when it was in the presence of a member of the imperial family. At last, he found the stone resting on a rocky ledge completely unprotected. "The assumption of this animal to believe I would be so easily contained that it should leave this prize unsheathed was foolish!" Montserrat snorted. He leaned over, picked up the empty chest that once contained his birthstone, and placed the stone back where it belonged. He then pressed his palm on the identification lock, but the lock was broken. Without a hiss of pressurized air, the chest's door could not close and lock; and would leave this planetary treasure—beyond any human being's comprehension—revealed and unprotected.

"The Darrn must have thought that if I had fallen at its ambush, it could have come back for the stone before its departure," Montserrat mused.

Montserrat deduced the Darrn had activated the Hunter because it must have felt it would need a backup legion to invade the planet. How long the device had been transmitting was unknown, and the risk it posed Montserrat was not willing to take. Montserrat had hoped the cave's walls and his cloaking it would have been enough to block the faint beacon signal from the ship after all these years, but now, he knew he must leave at once. He grabbed a lash pistol from a storage box that had been tossed away behind a patch of rocks, and gathered what he could find useful before he vaporized the area. He knew that leaving any evidence would jeopardize this planet even further. Standing safely outside of the cave, Montserrat pressed the detonator and the cave flashed with a sudden flare as all evidence of Montserrat's presence on Earth was fried instantly.

Having made his way across the city, Montserrat stopped at a motel and requested a room where he'd be isolated away from the rest of the tenants. He'd decided he would leave at dawn to eliminate any notice of his escape. He'd also picked up something to eat on his way to the motel and now lay on the bed in the dark staring out the window. He watched the different lights flicker and blink as the motel marquee illuminated his room. Extremely tired, he lay there with his eyes drooping while being hypnotized by the lights which reminded him of the Imperial Palace. He began to remember a thought that he had tried to forget.

2. THE SECRET

As the Queen had exited her observation dome tired and drained from the day's activities, she ducked into her secret passage to avoid the commoners and onlookers of the empire who may have wanted to detain her with accolades for her son, Montserrat. She pressed the hidden button elaborately concealed on a bejeweled statue of a muscular warrior wielding a sword. She looked upon the image and touched the face for a brief second before the sealed lock opened the door and a gust of cool air fluttered her flowing chiffon robes around her. She adjusted her collar and checked her appearance in the reflection of the mirror across the room. Unconsciously, her vanity was always first in her mind before entering a room. From one of the oldest royal lineages in Darr history, the Queen raised her shoulders, recalling she was a noble heir to the Pana Dynasty. Her father, highly decorated Lord Jeshua, was the ruler of Pana and the only trusted advisor to the late Emperor who had fought in the ancient Battle of Mugg. Lord Jeshua of Pana was also the late Emperor's best friend, and the Emperor had saved Jeshua's life on the battlefront more than once. As a token of loyalty, the Queen's father had promised her hand to the short, but scholarly, son of the Emperor when she came of age. Queen Aleon often wondered why she was the one who had to sacrifice her happiness out of the five princesses born in her family. She glanced at herself again, and for a brief second she saw her reflection of sadness. Upon seeing her inner-self revealed, she was disgusted with her weakness and straightened herself up to a more regal expression. She would not show her feelings to anyone, especially her husband. She walked down the hidden corridor and came out onto the landing of the private stairwell to Regent's Hall, avoiding the many passersby who would have stopped her. She began to walk up the stairs when she was distracted by a female voice.

"Queen Aleon, your young prince has taken the gauntlet again!" Lady Dreann exclaimed with a courtsy while rushing to the side of her Queen. "You must be very proud of him! That is his tenth victory for the Imperial champion!"

Still catching her breath, Lady Dreann, the daughter of the late arena champion Valnass, lifted the train to the Queen's flowing gown, as the Queen and her maiden entered Regent's Hall. The Queen sighed heavily and smiled at her lady in waiting, but her eyes confirmed to Lady Dreann that Queen Aleon was not truly happy.

"His victories at such a young age show he is truly thy son," the maiden whispered, as she put her hand on her Queen's elbow for support.

"Yes, he has the traits of a future Emperor! I cannot keep him in my skirt-tails any longer, for the Emperor wants him to fight the Great Darrn in the Cathedral of Cyclo. It is the only hope of retaining the throne of power," Queen Aleon said with a scowl of loss and longing.

"You do not think the Emperor's son can defeat the Darrn?" Lady Dreann asked.

Queen Aleon froze and stared at her lady in waiting, her quiet reserve now shattered. "You know as well as I that Montserrat is not the Emperor's son!" she blurted out angrily. "He holds the birthstone only by name—not by the Emperor's blood. A son by that sniveling slob called an emperor would be a disappointing slug like his father. I did the only thing I could to save our kingdom!" She confessed as her eyes grew moist.

"Oh dear Queen, my father loved you with all his soul and being! What you did for him he could never repay; even at his death in the arena, his loyalty was only for you. You gave him a son with a future and a throne to rule justly, not just a son to fight in the arena," Lady Dreann quietly said as she comforted the Queen.

"Montserrat has too much of your father's blood running through his veins, Dreann. I have shown him love of the arts, and I educated him in diplomacy to be a brilliant ruler. What good has it done? Where does he spend his time? In battle! All my love couldn't keep the fire in his soul contained. Now he must fight for his birthright or lose it to those smelly beasts. If it is lost, damnation on Darr will be inevitable for the next fifty years if not longer!" The Queen exclaimed while stifling an urge to sob uncontrollably. "Yes, indeed, your half-brother is *truly* the son of your father, Valnass!"

Montserrat had been standing behind the tall Regent Hall doors. He watched as his mother walked past him and into the royal court accompanied by his half-sister whom he didn't know existed. He couldn't get the name Valnass out of his head. He stood shocked as this realization sunk in that Valnass, the greatest warrior of all the history of Darr, was his . . . father!

He couldn't believe the revealed truth he'd just overheard from his mother. It must be why she had taken Dreann as her lady in waiting; they were never apart. "Could it be true?" Montserrat thought. "Could I truly be her half-brother? What about my father, the Emperor? I always knew I was nothing like the Emperor, but he had shown me so much love. Does he know? Should I tell him?" the young prince asked himself as he struggled with knowing the truth.

"Gods above, what should I do?" he prayed to himself. Slowly he walked towards his quarters, and as Montserrat entered his room, the great birthstone's gleam was blinding. He felt as though his insides had been ripped out. He suddenly hated that stone, but he hated the mess his mother had gotten him into even more.

3. DREAMS OF THE FATHER

Even here on Earth, Montserrat still had bitter feelings toward his birthstone. As he walked toward his motel room's bathroom to take a shower, he saw the low glow of the stone under his garments lying on the table. The stone was calling to him. He threw a towel he found on the shelf over the stone and dropped onto the bed forgetting about a shower. He was just so tired. As uncomfortable as the motel bed was, Montserrat drifted off into a deep sleep, where he was once again on Darr.

"Master, your father wishes to see you," whispered a familiar voice which had crept into the mind of the young prince. Montserrat was deep in thought; otherwise, he would have sensed this presence. It startled him.

Krueck, the viceroy to the prince, was from Thrans, a telepathic-populated planet devoted to serving the empire as a governing representative. He was also Montserrat's most trusted friend. Since childhood, Krueck had been his only confidant and at a young age with Krueck's guidance, the prince had acquired the skills to open his own thoughts telepathically. They were like brothers and Montserrat needed someone to talk to, but now did not feel like the right time.

"Thanks K," the Prince said as he walked toward the dressing room. Montserrat wondered if Krueck knew who the prince's real paternal father was because of their telepathic ability.

After dressing in flying gear, Montserrat proceeded to his private airship parked outside his balcony. He would love to levitate there without having to take an aircraft, but his father would never permit it in public. He slid into the seat, ignited the engine, and shot off to Darr's City of the Clouds.

Hovering in the sky, the palace city was highly guarded and the safest place to stay in the whole emporium. After receiving clearance from the Trans to enter the city, Montserrat proceeded to the grand entrance. The sun was illuminating through the clouds creating a red afternoon glow that was caressing the beautiful quartz walls and the limestone steps to the spectacular entry.

The air was crisp on this floating masterpiece of land as he landed his craft and jumped out. On the steps, the cooing of the Argus beckoned but as he walked closer to the steps, the Argus with their bright blue and green plumage lifted off to a safe distance. Montserrat thought this sight was akin to a symphony of slow motion. The smell of lilacs wafted past his face as the ornate birds gracefully glided to their desired landing pods. Making short time of his ascent to the gold and jeweled encrusted doors, Montserrat also noticed the Trans; like a swarm of bees, they were everywhere—from the shadows to the entry of the palace.

To the Trans guards, Montserrat gave his imperial hand salute by raising his two fingers in a peace sign just over his heart and brushing them over his chest plate. They quickly cleared a path as Montserrat remembered how the swift and watchful Trans had come to Darr from the planet Transia, two parsecs away from his home-world. The Trans could be overwhelming to an intruder facing a crowd of them. They could even surround an enemy in seconds with their weapons in a way that no adversary could escape. Never fearful, they would fight to the death until victorious or eliminated, and never surrender or give up. He was thankful their allegiance had been to the royal family for more than five centuries; they lived solely to serve the Emperor, and this fact had never wavered.

Entering the stateroom, Montserrat arrived just as the senate forum ended. A few dignitaries congratulated the prince on his latest victory and his flourishing reputation.

"My son," the Emperor said in a pleasing tone, as he floated quickly down from the balcony to embrace his son.

"You know, Father . . . levitating is against Imperial law" Montserrat commented as the Emperor pressed against him.

Montserrat smelled the scent of sandalwood which was a comfort to him; it was a pleasant aroma and caused Montserrat to hold his father for a fraction longer than normal.

"What would you do if the Emperor found out?" Montserrat said jokingly to the man in front of him.

The Emperor snorted as he put on a firm but false scowl, "Oh, I can break a few of my own rules now and then. Just don't tell your mother!" jovially whispered the Emperor, as he took his son's arm.

"My son, you have done it again; the royal court must have a ball in honor of your triumph," the excited Emperor mentioned as they walked. "Tell me all of the details. Did you look him in the eye as you twisted your blade in his heart?" he said with a ferocious look of morbid interest on his aged and puffy face.

"Yes, Father, just as you told me," Montserrat laughed, as he escorted his father onto the next platform.

"By all the gods, not since the time of Valnass have I seen such a battle! Five Darrn, you remind me so much of my old friend . . ." the Emperor rejoiced.

With these words Montserrat glanced back at his father, noticing the Emperor appeared conflicted in saying these words.

"Don't you have more business to deal with, Father?" he interrupted. "I don't want to keep you from your duties," Montserrat commented as he helped the Emperor sit down.

"Nonsense my son, the Emperor is never too busy for his son. We must celebrate!" the Emperor said smiling as he patted Montserrat on the shoulder. "And I have a surprise for you," he added as he squirmed in his cushioned throne.

Knowing what the Emperor was about to proclaim, Montserrat blurted out suddenly, "I cannot fight the Great Darrn in the Cathedral," Montserrat declared to the Emperor.

Surprised, the Emperor's smile disappeared with his happy disposition. "You can't, huh? You have to, by law! The heir to the throne must compete to hold our place at the kingdom's gate. Without this, we will lose all of our holdings and the opposed victors can claim their place on the throne, banishing us for the decades of five!" raged the Emperor. The Emperor stood up from the throne and frowned at Montserrat. "Why can't you fight then?" he asked in a stern tone.

"Valnass protected your throne. Why can't we have someone else hold mine?" Montserrat retorted.

The Emperor stepped down to face the young prince. "Valnass was my best friend, and he was like a brother to me. Because of my health and the love my father had for him, he was permitted to take my place. The Great Darrn also thought they would be victorious over Valnass because he was unknown as a gladiator," the Emperor said solemnly as the memory of his friend became fresh.

"However, Valnass defeated the Great Darrn. Even when he continued to do so—though mortally wounded—before the final great fight in the Cathedral of Cyclo. That is when the Darrn used treachery by using a tainted blade. Though Valnass had defeated his greatest enemy, the Great Darrn, the poison from the Darrn's hook took the life of Valnass a few days after the event. The Darrn thought that this would assure their victory in the next battle of power."

The Emperor lowered his head at his next comment in hidden shame. "I would not have survived the first round. It took six of those beasts to take Valnass. You are our only hope. YOU ARE THE CHAMPION! Remember . . . YOU ARE THE CHAMPION, YOU ARE THE CHAMPION!"

4. THE VISITOR

Though asleep, hearing his father's echoing words roused Montserrat from his rest whereupon he wiped the perspiration from his face. Getting up, he walked to the motel room's window and looked out into the night. He could see the city lights and a few automobiles creeping down the freeway making their way to their midnight destinations. Montserrat rubbed his eyes as he looked out again into the night sky to verify he was just dreaming about his father. There was no sign of anyone around the motel, but Montserrat felt the urgency to pack up his things.

"Hello my Prince," he unexpectedly heard in his tired state.

He spun around in a crouched fighting stance when he heard the voice continue, "You are still as fast as the mighty cats on Mecan."

A smile instantly washed over Montserrat's face as he straightened and walked to the door and opened it. He knew who was at the door and was grateful: it was Krueck, his childhood friend who Montserrat hadn't seen since before he'd left for Earth.

They embraced and Montserrat noticed how Krueck had not changed or aged since last he'd last seen Krueck.

"It's good to see you, my friend. I've missed you," the Prince said aloud. He moved to let his friend enter. "What has happened on Darr?"

Montserrat then asked as he turned, retrieved his case, and began to pack. "A Darrn attacked me yesterday in the city just south of here. It had a Hunter which I've destroyed, but you and I must leave before this planet becomes prey to the Darrn."

"That's why I'm here, my Prince," Krueck clearly explained as he helped to gather Montserrat's things. "The Darrn have committed Backtar."

Backtar was the first attack to break peace in the harmony of Darr. Imperial Law states that if retaliation is not launched, the throne is forfeited and the attacker is placed in power. By engaging in Backtar, the Darrn have called out the Emperor to fight in the Cathedral of Cyclo.

"I left so there wouldn't be a chance for the Darrn to challenge the throne simply because then there wouldn't be an arena 'champion' to fight *for* the seat of the Kingdom. With me as champion gone, all must stay as it is. That is why I left—to keep things as they are," Montserrat said. "After all these years, they declared Backtar to lure me back to the arena and if I don't go back, they claim the throne. If I do go back, I'll have to fight. But why are they sending Darrn out to bring me back?" Montserrat asked as he started toward the door.

Krueck grabbed his friend's arm. "They won't bring you back!" he exclaimed aloud. "The Darrn have been sent out to terminate you, Montserrat, and claim you tried to attack them instead of returning to fight. This will secure their position for the royal seat," he said slowly letting go of the Prince's arm. "If you don't return, they will attack the Palace ag___!" Krueck fell silent. Now holding his tongue, he looked down awkwardly toward the baggage.

"Krueck! You were going to say, 'Again,' weren't you? What has happened? I must know!" Montserrat demanded.

Krueck didn't look at the prince as he told him how the Darrn had attacked the Palace, destroyed part of the arena, abducted both Queen

Aleon and Lady Dreann, and were holding them captive on the planet of Minrall.

"We could rescue them there on the way home!" Krueck said excitedly, now looking at the prince intently.

Montserrat asked if the Emperor and the guards had tried to rescue the two women. Krueck explained the Emperor had tried, but to no avail: the Minrall had taken allegiance with the Darrn and all rescue attempts so far had been futile. With the Minrall's cunning chameleon skills, they had been sending the Trans on false chases, always resulting in ambushes.

"We must leave, my Prince. You're not safe here," Krueck said as he walked out of the room into the night with the Prince in front of him. As they walked around the corner of the motel, Montserrat was astonished to see that Krueck's ship was a Darrn war shuttle.

He whirled around to ask Krueck to explain this ship when a hulking arm of rock struck him. It took Montserrat completely by surprise and had thrown him against the exterior wall, knocking the wind out of him. At first he was stunned and couldn't find his balance, but his keen intellect was intact. It was a Minrall disguised to look like his friend Krueck. Montserrat was too dazed to fight back. As his eyes tried to focus, the last thing Montserrat could remember were bright green blasts lighting up the alley.

Waking from a distant noise, Montserrat suddenly became aware he was on an examining table, and his head was splitting with throbbing pain. He closed his eyes when he heard the door swish open behind him. The visitor moved to a monitor that was illuminating some vital signs. Montserrat turned to see who had entered the room and could see something familiar about this person. "It looks like Krueck, but why would the Minrall have changed back to his friend's form?" Montserrat thought as he realized he was not bound. "Why am I not tied up?" he asked himself.

"You will never be tied up, my Prince," said a voice from the visitor. He walked up beside the Prince and said, "I'm not a Minrall; I am the real Krueck, my Prince. I arrived just as the Minrall gave you that love tap," he said jokingly as he helped Montserrat sit up.

"How do I know *you* are not an impostor?" Montserrat barked, as he clutched his throbbing head and stepped into defensive positioning.

Krueck answered in a calming voice, "Why would I have allowed you to be free in my ship and be alone without any restraints?"

"As a trick!" Montserrat exclaimed as he began to breathe rapidly to generate an energy blast. He wasn't about to go down without a fight. "How do I know you are not a Minrall? What proof can you give to me to believe you?" Montserrat demanded, stalling as he gained more energy.

Telepathically, Krueck then projected a name in Montserrat's head, "Gojii." Montserrat at once felt the sharp pang in his stomach as he heard this name. Gojii was Montserrat's woman from the Chazen sector. She was a Giron, and the Girons are forbidden on Darr because of their ability to hypnotize anyone with their erotic beauty and twisted words. Being around the Giron would cause anybody to become obsessed with them while the Giron's only interest is in getting information from their victims to sell to the highest bidder.

Montserrat's eyes widened as this name opened a history he had tried so hard to bury. The sentence for anyone caught with a Giron—or even to know of anyone in contact with one—is execution. The two men had sworn to secrecy about Gojii with a blood bond. This was, indeed, Krueck—his truest friend and companion.

Krueck explained how he too had picked up on the Hunter signal transmitting from Earth, most likely the one in the cave left by the Darrn. At the same time, long-range communications also disclosed a Minrall ship was tracking the Hunter's transmission to Earth. Undetected, Krueck used the Minrall ship's plasma burn to follow them to Earth. Because it landed, Krueck assumed Montserrat must be nearby, so he, too, put down nearby. When Krueck came around from behind the Minrall's ship, he saw Montserrat exiting the motel room. The Minrall then transformed itself and attacked the Prince. That was when Krueck opened fire and destroyed the Minrall and their ship.

"In short, the Minrall animals wanted to use you for a bargaining tool with the Darrn," Krueck concluded. Montserrat patted his friend on the shoulder in unspoken gratitude.

After a few hours of briefing on what had been happening back home, Montserrat realized almost everything the Minrall had told him was correct. The only thing untrue was that not all attempts to save Queen Aleon and Lady Dreann had been in vain. In fact, Krueck and his team had just captured a Darrn freighter traveling to the Onard Colony two weeks ago. It was a slave freighter carrying fifty-six women from Darr, but one slave was the Lady Dreann in a suspended stasis box. She was reported to have been causing trouble for the Darrn by escaping from her cell to signal any pursuers from Darr.

"Is she all right?" the Prince asked alarmed.

"The animals! The Darrn had severed her hand to punish her and warn her she was to behave. She is a bit bruised but will survive. She's now safe in the medical chamber on our ship. It's expected to dock shortly; then we'll transport her to the infirmary. She's in a stasis gurney, but her life signs are strong." Krueck commented. "She is just like her father—she never gives up," Krueck said reassuringly.

Montserrat, already feeling guilty for leaving his mother and sister unprotected, became furious at this distressing news. He struck his fist on the console next to where he'd been standing.

"I want to see her when she is able," Montserrat sternly said to Krueck. "let's get to Darrn!"

By early morning, they had reached the Darr space dock. From here, Montserrat was able to see all the moons of Darr fade before he stepped out on the platform. He took in a deep breath and whispered to himself, "I'm home."

5. THE RETURN TO DARR

The Trans were out on training maneuvers. Montserrat could see his emperor father in battle uniform standing on a floating platform alongside the half-ling, Minnion, Master of the Guard. Together they were observing the troops who were preparing for a possible Darrn strike. Montserrat stepped on a hover podium to meet up with the Emperor and his entourage. The Emperor was talking to Minnion when he noticed Montserrat's approach. He let out an obvious expression of excitement followed by a deep sigh as he saw Montserrat step from the hover podium onto their platform and bow in the traditional way. The Emperor stood up, and they hesitated briefly before they fell into an embrace.

This man was all Montserrat knew as a father, and whether he was or not, Montserrat loved him as any child would love a parent. The length of their embrace touched Montserrat deeply and tears welled up in his eyes.

"Father, I have missed you," Montserrat declared as he held his Emperor's forearms in his own. "Tell me of the progress on finding mother," he implored as he nodded to the Master of the Guard and thinking to himself how hideous this creature looked.

The Master of the Guard cleared his raspy voice with a foul rumble of phlegm which made it sound as if he needed to expel some mucus. Minnion tried to smile with his fanged mouth, yet it made him look even more frightening. Montserrat momentarily thought Minnion's grin looked rather sinister and forced. "I wonder if this animal is as loyal as everyone thinks he is?" the Prince pondered as he turned to address his Emperor.

"I just arrived with the survivors on the slave freighter. Lady Dreann was aboard, but she was severely injured as a result of her last campaign to escape. The freighter is intact and was brought here in case we want to use it as a transit into Darrn space for a rescue mission," Montserrat informed his father.

The Master of the Guard cleared his throat again in another attempt to dislodge whatever he had in his throat.

"Minnion, do you have something to say to my son?" the Emperor asked in response to Minnion's repeated choking on his own phlegm.

"Yes, my lord. I would like to ask how the Prince plans on executing his rescue of the Queen, for it may be too . . . dangerous for the young prince," he crackled through the mucus.

"Now, Minnion, we can go over all that later," interrupted the Emperor as he shot a sharp look towards his master guardsman.

The Emperor continued this stare as he pulled his son onto Montserrat's hover podium to leave. "We must discuss where Monty has been…what he's been up to. Do you have any needs, my boy?" he asked gliding away with his son.

The Prince looked back to the battlement platform briefly and saw Minnion's eyes narrow in a chilling glare before the Master of the Guard turned in sudden haste, causing his uniform cape to flutter in the wind.

Montserrat turned back toward the Emperor who had stopped talking and was staring at his son with great intensity. "My son…you've changed; you're no longer a child," he mumbled as he put on a reassuring smile and straightened his robes. "I've missed you immensely, and Darr needs you now more than ever."

Montserrat could see his father was nervous because the Emperor would always fumble with his robes when something was on his mind. Now standing close to his father, Montserrat could see how he had aged. He was heavier, and he had let his hair grow longer. If Montserrat didn't know any better, his Emperor would just say it was dirty, making it appear longer. "He must be distraught over mother," Montserrat thought as he grabbed the controls of the podium.

They had begun to dock at the palace when a guard approached them. The Emperor took a holographic telegram from the Trans guard and dismissed the guard with a wave of his hand. The guard's eyes were almost clear, indicating danger.

"What is the matter, Father?" Montserrat asked, as he moved to the stairs to let his father step off of the podium.

"Most disturbing news, I'm afraid. I must meet in private with a visitor in the Great Hall." explained the Emperor as he started up the stairs in a hurry. Clustered together nearby, the Argos took off in a flurry as the two men rushed up the entrance almost trampling the exotic birds. Upon entering through the great doorway, Montserrat stopped and looked as the Emperor and the Trans disappeared around a corner leading to the Great Hall. Knowing it would be awhile before he could continue his conversation with his father, the young prince turned and decided it was time to visit his sibling.

6. THE ALLIANCE

Montserrat entered the infirmary and asked to see Lady Dreann. The orderly, a young Neptic monk whom his father had imported from the medical planet in the Latrobe system, motioned to the young prince with his webbed hand to follow him. He led Montserrat through the Nan organic ward. Montserrat followed him looking at the Neptic's elongated hands as they swayed in a movement reminding him of the tailfins of giant goldfish in the Emperor's private meditation ponds. Montserrat caught sight of the flared gills that were on the opalescent skinned orderly. He wondered, with surprise, why he hadn't noticed them before—knowing they'd come to Darr from an underwater world. As Montserrat entered Lady Dreann's large hospital room, he was amazed to see how many orderlies attended her.

Above his head, he observed many floating humidifiers designed to resemble scurrying schools of fish as they maneuvered around hanging lanterns and expelled a continuous salty mist. The room's ocean murals and the humidifiers created a moisturizing ocean-like environment much like being on a platform overlooking the Sea of Nepti. The ever-present dampness was for the comfort and health of the monks. The mist aided in the replacement of their lost orthopedic anatomy and neurologic tissue, for without the humidifiers, the Neptics would age prematurely and gradually become dehydrated organisms. He recalled a time he had studied the benefits of the medical breakthroughs these species had brought to his father's Empire years ago. Today though, the caregiving Neptics gurgled a melodious sound to one another that reminded the Prince of a familiar lullaby. The sound made the prince relax and at the same time rejuvenated him as he began to walk with a renewed step. Montserrat was so engrossed with his thoughts and observations, he hadn't noticed he was now beside his half-sister's bed.

Lady Dreann smiled and tried to attempt a reverent bow. But her head pounded from a previous concussion inflicted by the abusive Darrn, so five orderlies supported her as she moved to greet her younger brother.

"Hello, my sister!" Montserrat enthusiastically whispered as he bent across her bed to kiss her cheek.

Realizing he'd never called her sister before, Lady Dreann's eyes widened as he pulled away to right himself. She looked up at the prince and saw her father's features in her half-brother's face. "How long have you known?" she asked as she moved to get comfortable in her bed.

Montserrat looked down at her with an anguished look in his eyes. "Since before I left to go to Earth. I have been living this dream hoping that it was a lie, but I asked for a sample of our DNA to be compared. It came back positive."

He quickly looked away as he finished this statement. His half-sister saw the look of sorrow in his face knowing he had tried to mask his feelings from her.

"I need to find my mother," he said abruptly, hoping to shift their conversation.

The orderlies gathered around the room chanting a wave of hums and clicks as they began collecting information. As they recorded their information, two more Neptic monks walked in with a tray of bandages and ointments.

The faint smell of the healing ointments reminded Montserrat of a trip he and his parents took to the Isle of Exocoe. The Exocon, Giant flying fish, inhabited the island; unfortunately, the fish were exploited almost to extinction because their wings were a natural fiber stronger than many metals. Useful in the military as well as in medicine, the fiber could be used to manufacture flexible lightweight armor or as an organic balm to re-grow human anatomy. The smell of the fish salve was nauseating, and Montserrat recalled how he would heave with convulsions when his family would find an Exocon poached for its wings. Shortly after their trip, the Emperor declared the isle an endangered environment and the poaching ceased. Only controlled harvesting was now in place on Exocoe, but the smell was unmistakable even now. As the orderlies began to change the dressing on Lady Dreann's wrist, the young prince had to cover his nose as he watched. He was expecting to see a miraculous re-growth from the ointment, but Lady Dreann's wrist and hand still looked both deformed and gangrenous.

After the monks left, Lady Dreann wanted to be cheerful saying to the prince, "It's hard to believe that this hand is completely re-grown. The salve they administered has a replenishing factor that aids in rapid organic growth."

"It smells disgusting!" Montserrat interrupted as he moved back to find some relief by an air vent. "Besides, I didn't come here to discuss medical breakthroughs; I came here to give you my condolences, and to wish you a speedy recovery."

He moved closer to the vent as a brisk odorous current passed by his face. "I'll be leaving in the morning to find my mother. There's been word that she may have been hidden on a planet festering with the Darrn," he blurted out. He had now regained his composure after receiving a fresh burst of air.

"I want to go!" Dreann cried with surprising strength as she straightened herself in her bed. "I wasn't her child, but I loved her as one would!" she said, stifling an urge to cry.

"You can help me better by staying here. That way, I'll know you're safe," he said affectionately. "Besides, I'll need you to keep me informed, too; something is not right here." Gesturing to her to talk lower, he reluctantly moved from the vent and stepped up to the side of her bed. "I feel a conspiracy is underway here in the palace, but I must leave to see if my hunch is correct," Montserrat whispered to her bending down to kiss her again. Then offering her an encouraging hug, he said, "I'll be back soon, and we'll have a lot to catch up on, Sis."

Upon leaving the hospital, Montserrat walked toward the conservatory to meet with Krueck who was charting the best course to the planet Mugg. As Montserrat walked down the corridor, he remembered a secret Imperial study that was nearby. He entered his code password and the door hissed open.

Montserrat came here alone when he was younger in order to get away from the typical royal banter and scheduled engagements. He walked up to the familiar computer console and found that it had recently been accessed. As he opened the files with his royal codes, he also discovered his mission files had been viewed and copied to a memory crystal. He was alarmed to see that even his personal files had been copied. He knew at once that whoever had opened this console had to have very high royal clearance.

Only three others had this type of access: his mother and father, and Minnion. But why had this been so important? His parents had no reason to copy his files. However, Minnion was not on the prince's most favorite servant list; in fact, he had believed Minnion to be a spy for quite some time.

Even as a little boy, Montserrat never trusted him. Many times throughout his life, Montserrat had felt that his father's Master of the Guard was shifty and unconvincingly innocent. Montserrat wondered if it was the beast who was spying on him now and who had also looked through his personal files.

With no time left to lose, Montserrat looked around and spotted what he was looking for: a small secret door, concealing a small cache which he opened. Then pulling his birthright stone out from his pocket, he noticed it felt hot. He liked the warm comforting feeling, yet he shook his head as he realized he wasn't to be comfortable—he needed to be cautious. He put the stone into the secret compartment knowing that this was a spot no other person knew about.

Within half an hour, he had reached the freighter bound for the breeding planet of the Darrn known as Mugg. Setting the course as he prepared the ship for its departure, he was going to level the planet Mugg with all his ship's might.

7. THE STOWAWAY

After Montserrat had left her bedside, Lady Dreann collected her clothes and slipped them under her gown. An orderly came back to her bedside and began to fuss with her bandages. She asked the Neptic monk if she could use the restroom, and it tried to assist her. "I believe I can manage," she said as she pulled away from the monk. "Thank you," she commented as she walked slowly toward the restroom to her right. She looked back and saw that the monk had turned away to straighten her bed. Unnoticed and with a quick pace, she instead turned left through the hospital exit.

As the Lady Dreann walked to the Royal transports, she had been thinking of Montserrat's comments about the Queen and her decision to keep her secret from the Prince. Lady Dreann believed the Queen had acted rationally as the Prince would have caused a commotion at the time.

"Montserrat was always so impulsive," she remembered to herself, "and things haven't changed much. He was extremely upset about this news today."

She had vowed in blood to the Queen that she would never tell the prince of this scandal. She was now greatly relieved to realize she no longer had this burden on her shoulders.

Dreann had, however, also learned that her father, the Great Valnass, was a royal descendant. To Dreann and Montserrat's misfortune, the Queen had disappeared before Dreann could get the full details on their father's lineage.

Hurrying toward the transport tubes, the Trans suddenly came out from the shadows and stopped Lady Dreann in her tracks. She jumped and automatically crouched to a fighting stance, but not because of their sudden appearance. She was used to them appearing from nowhere, but at this moment, she was deep in thought and with a narrow escape from her recent abduction, the Trans had simply caught her off guard.

Lady Dreann gave them the imperial salute, and they asked her for her heading. She presented them with a royal Form of Departure and explained that she was to be placed on the Prince's freighter undetected. The Trans gave her acknowledgement and let her proceed past them. As she passed, two of the Trans looked at one another, and one of them turned and began speaking indistinctly in his communicator.

When Lady Dreann entered the transport tube, she noticed an unexpected change in the guard's eyes. For her, these semi-transparent creatures had been harder to read lately, especially since the Darrn attack. She'd always felt they were not as loyal as they were supposed to have been, but they had never done anything against royalty since she had been alive; she just felt weird about them sometimes, and this was one of those times.

The tube closed and the lights switched to red. In seconds, she was cruising at light speed to arrive at the shipyard. She was planning on boarding Montserrat's freighter secretly until it launched, and that way, the Prince would have to take her along. Lady Dreann began to chuckle a little as she thought, she too, was impulsive in a similar way to Montserrat.

When the transport tube doors opened, Lady Dreann walked to the dock where the freighter was waiting, and snuck unseen into the freighter through the cargo doors as supplies were loaded for the trip. She slipped through another inner cargo door that led into the ship, and found a vacant chamber in the hull. Now, as she waited and looked around at her surroundings, the memory of her abduction was fresh in her mind.

When Lady Dreann walked into the chamber, she realized there was another open door in the room, so she put her cloak down and strolled to the other side of the room. She picked up a torn piece of fine silk she'd noticed on the floor, not unlike the material of the Queen's wardrobe. Still pondering its origin, she then entered the hall from the newly discovered door. An odor assaulted her nostrils as Lady Dreann moved closer to the many other chambers in the wing. Suddenly, she realized this was the ship the Darrn had hijacked to abduct the Queen, and the area the Queen had been held in as a captive. As Lady Dreann reached the door, her healing hand was now on fire with pain. She wondered if there was a problem with her new hand because it was so odd and so sudden. Then when Lady Dreann came around the corner of the doorway, she stopped, rigid in the horror that was before her.

She braced herself by leaning against a cabinet that must have also been used as a restraint. Lady Dreann became ill; she had a vivid mental picture of what this room was used for, and it made her pale in disgust. The walls, covered in blood and secretions, were crawling with a maggot-type parasites feeding on the writing that had dried, but which had once been dripping from the wall.

It was all becoming crystal clear, and the message on the wall made her shudder with this realization. It was now apparent to her who was responsible for this treachery. She needed to tell her brother immediately even if it would cause him to be upset with her. She turned around suddenly to leave, but it was too late to duck as the tranquilizer struck her right shoulder. She began to drop while also vaguely feeling invisible arms catching her. Her last memory was a faint, clear, aquamarine-blue stare.

8. PLANET MUGG

Montserrat believed his assault on Mugg was going well, maybe *too* well. But as he moved closer, he dismissed his thoughts; it was going to be over soon whether he found his mother or not. The stench was revolting and together with Krueck and their small group of mercenaries, the team was having a hard time breathing without the urge of dry heaves and vomiting.

As the group shuffled through the rubble of bones and greasy sludge, they noticed birthing cubicles in the trash. Newborn Darrn infants were milking on their sleeping mothers' multiple teats. Some infants were trying to walk, but the sludge on the ground made it difficult for the beasts to get a sure footing, and they would topple into the heaps of carcasses and garbage.

The rescue party was getting wearisome and Montserrat was desperate to find his mother, the Queen. A waking Darrn mother struggled to her feet, her litter still attached and milking. With a rumble from her throat, the children instantly dropped to the ground as if they knew her warning. However, one of her cubs still clung to her; without any mercy, she slapped the nursing beast off of her as if it was a pestering insect. The infant beast spiraled into a pile of broken objects and didn't move leaving Montserrat dismayed with this species' barbaric nature.

The Darrn mother dropped into a defensive stance between the intruders and her litter, as her protective instincts took over. The angered mother then rose up and towered over the group of fighters. Reaching eighteen feet tall, she bore her yellow fangs and sharp claws as she bellowed in a raspy voice, "How dare you come here, human!" She moved closer and croaked out, "You will not leave here alive!"

With her last rattling breath, she lunged at the Prince but to her surprise, Krueck appeared with a lash-blade and struck her first. The hot blade severed through her as if she were made of wax. The beast gurgled on her blood as the fatal wound choked the life out of her. She dropped to the floor writhing with spasms. The group continued their battle as they stepped over the corpse avoiding not to step in the pooling acidic blood. They fanned out, and began incinerating almost everything that moved with a lash-torch. Then just before giving one final burst of flame from his weapon, Montserrat moved passed a pile of rotting flesh when he was startled by a soft voice.

"Monty? My son, is that you?" the Queen murmured in a soft but strained voice.

Montserrat turned to see his mother and gasped in horror as he saw what had become of his beautiful mother.

"They will pay," he thought as he rushed to her side.

Once a beautiful elegant woman with poise and grace, she was now stripped of her dignity in the most revolting way. Queen Aleon lay there obese and greasy from the sludge that was all over her clothes and matted hair. The Queen was heavily drugged, causing her to be disorientated and delirious. She had been raped by the Darrn and had been left in this "nursery of filth" to give birth to their spawn.

The anatomy of a Darrn was completely different from human. Although their DNA was compatible, they gave birth to litters of six to eight offspring, and the intense growth of the Darrn fetus is much greater than for a normal human. The beasts had to sever the Queen's spine to accommodate the growth of her placenta. So now his mother looked like a huge slug with multiple lumps. Her lower body hung lifeless as the Darrns' fetuses stretched and rolled inside the massive folds of her birthing sack. For Montserrat this was a sick joke, yet the hideous animals felt it was an appropriate sentence for the ruling Queen of Darr.

The Queen tried to hide as Montserrat approached. "Don't come any closer," she sobbed as she pulled a makeshift drape over her rancid body.

She had grown so large that she couldn't manage to even lift her limbs, and she shook with the effort. "I don't want you to remember me this way my son. I am lost!" Giving up her attempt to hide, she began to cry convulsively.

Montserrat climbed the pile to where she was and embraced her; they both began to weep as she returned his love.

"Oh, my son, it's a godsend to see you," she muttered as she held on tighter, "I have become what we hate most!"

"No, Mother, we will help you," he explained as he wiped the dirt from her face. "We'll destroy this vermin for what they have done, and you'll recover," he said with a majestic air about him yet still full of disgust and hatred. "You are our Queen; you *have* to make it! Don't give up."

She smiled briefly and coughed, "My dear son, I love you so much, but I am already dead."

She touched his hand and whispered, "I cannot live my life after what has happened to me. I have only lasted this long in hopes of seeing you again." She kissed his hand and held it close to her face. "I loved your father very much, and I want you to know this."

37

Montserrat interrupted her, "Which father do you mean, Mother?" he said as he looked at her with kindness.

She was shocked, but on her face he knew she had figured out his meaning. "Monty, I loved the father you know and the father you could have known. I wanted to be sure that the Empire had a chance of survival," she sobbed as she tried to convince him. Then anger washed over her and she spat, "This is what I deserve for what I have done. I have endangered you— and this, I fear— was a trap," she gasped as her eyes fixed on an approaching horror. "Son, I have found proof of a conspiracy…"

A crunching sound came from behind them, and Montserrat's eyes narrowed; he whirled around and blasted the beast as it approached stealthily but clumsily. His blast burst through the invader's chest and he called to his guards to line up in a fighting formation. He handed his mother his dagger for protection—though he knew it would do her no good—and began to blast the incoming vermin that was attacking them.

His crew of fighters appeared, and they pushed the beasts back into a cave destroying everything in their way. Montserrat gave orders to his soldiers and told Krueck to watch over his mother. They managed to make the beasts retreat, and then he blasted the cave's entrance trapping the beasts within. Knowing more Darrn would close in soon, this was his window of opportunity to retreat.

Montserrat ran to his mother but stopped in his tracks. Krueck grabbed him and tried to turn the Prince away, but it was too late. His mother had used her last bit of energy and had stabbed every lump in her engorged body; then she had taken her own life. Montserrat roared with grief as anger took over his actions. He was incensed with fury, and his eyes were like two molten stones blazing in the darkness. He was in pain, and he wanted to make sure someone else felt his pain.

Montserrat grabbed his projectile rifle, strode up a pile of rubble, and fired three stingers into the area where they had trapped their attackers. The stingers were concentrated mini napalm lethally intensified by an electrical charge. As the rock wall collapsed by the blast, the sight was nauseating. The small entrance illuminated like the opening to a furnace. The heat was overwhelming, and the sight of the writhing Darrn was grotesque as their skin and hair dripped off their charring bones. The inferno was a mystifying sight—everything moved so slowly until at last, no movement was detectable. Several moments had passed, and now the only noise was the sound of Krueck barking orders for the remaining crew to recon at the shuttle.

The crew had rescued those in their landing party who would make it back to Darr, and the remains of the Queen were brought aboard the shuttle and placed in a stasis chamber. Once the ship had been secured, the young prince then ordered his soldiers to set multiple cube-chargers before exiting the surface of the compound.

The look on the prince's face was one of such hatred that silence ruled the bridge of the ship. His emotions were ablaze and his eyes were in a wrathful daze as he breathed deeply and ravenously. While hovering in the upper atmosphere of Mugg, Montserrat glanced at his hand which was still gripping the dagger he had given his mother. He couldn't remember when he had picked it up, but now it was like the cold steel had become part of his arm. He looked back at his console and with a heavy sigh, the prince pressed the toggle. The cube-charges ignited, creating one final mega-blast which leveled and disintegrated everything within a fifty mile radius on the surface of Mugg. Without saying a word, he left the bridge and retreated to his private quarters for the remainder of their flight.

9. PORT HERMES

While the freighter landed on Port Hermes Medical Station, Montserrat's crew saw to the care of their wounded. It was a silent encounter as the remains of the Queen were prepared and presented in a stasis coffin to the Neptic surgeons who would restore the majestic beauty of the Queen before her final interment. Ignoring the rotting odor, the Prince oversaw every detail of the care and preservation of his mother. He sent a message to his father stating the accounts of their rescue mission, and asked for the burial rights to be delayed until his victory and return.

Later as he sat in his stateroom, he was remembering his mother's last words of a conspiracy and trap. In his heart he was positive it was his father's Master of the Guard, Minnion. There were too many negative factors about Minnion for it not to be him. Minnion had sought to know Montserrat's rescue plans, and if it hadn't been for his father's interruption, Minnion may have gotten the information he needed.

"My medical and personal records had been copied and reviewed, and I don't think my parents would have done that," Montserrat thought as he adjusted his battle cape worn in honor of his mother.

He remembered his father's constant wardrobe adjustments and grinned briefly as he fixed the collar. The Prince was now positive there was a conspiracy, and definitely a trap was being set for the Empire's defeat.

"The trap had to come from the inside. Obviously, it was Minnion!" Montserrat concluded as he resolvedly pounded his fist on the desk's console. "I'll make him confess!" Montserrat blurted out as he abruptly stood up.

He turned, and he was startled by the sight of a pair of blue aquamarine eyes in the corner of his entry way.

"What is it?" Montserrat snarled at the Trans guard.

His hand had slid to his side blade without the slightest thought. The guard advanced and handed the Prince a holographic note.

"Excuse the intrusion, my Lord, but we have a message from the Emperor," the guard whispered as he handed the note to the Prince. "We are to join the convoy at once which is headed to battle the planet Sikar." The guard stepped back and stared at the Prince with dark blue eyes. "I am sorry for the loss of our Queen, but I am happy to see you've returned my Lord. We are. . . I am hoping you will champion at the arena," the Trans said softly into his translator. The device gave the Trans a rattling, tinny voice. With that said, the Trans turned and disappeared as fast and quietly as a cat in the night.

Self-conscious of being cagy, the Prince looked questionably to where the guard had been standing. He did not like how the Trans came and went without any warning. "I'll have to mention to my father that the Trans take too many liberties," he thought to himself. Standing alone, he felt the ship dislodge from the landing platform then heard the increasing hum of the engines as it was thrust into space.

He looked at the note briefly. As the guard had mentioned, he was ordered to join the convoy and proceed to the planet Sikar. The Darrn were assembling an attack force, and the Emperor wanted him to lead the raid. The Emperor was sending Minnion to help with support. Montserrat sneered at this last part as he threw the message in his refuge incinerator. He was increasingly displeased with this partnership, so he telepathically summoned Krueck and requested his company to discuss his feelings.

Krueck arrived shortly after he was beckoned, and they sat together cerebrally discussing Montserrat's distrust and the conspiracy issues. Krueck listened and gave council. He, too, had felt a rift in the peace of this kingdom.

"I've been called out of court many times for various reasons! I felt that Minnion's dismissal of me was a way to keep me from hearing something covert," he added. Continuing, he said, "Many times upon my return to court, the other members would not brief me on the content of the court session I'd missed. It was as if they were ordered to keep silent!" He went on to explain how lately his engagements with the members of the court were far fewer than they had been just a year ago.

Their telepathic conversation was cut off when a Trans arrived with a note stating that they were approaching the convoy. The Master of the Guard's personal battle frigate had arrived for the Prince. He was to join Minnion for a briefing of the attack. Montserrat responded to the Trans with a salute, and then he turned to Krueck as the Trans made his leave.

"Do you want to help me uncover some answers?" he whispered as he put on his armor.

Krueck answered him telepathically, "Only if we are careful. Minnion scares the ghost out of me every time he looks at me!"

Montserrat laughed and grabbed Krueck's shoulder. "At times, he scares me too, but suspicion is now on *our* side!" he mentally communicated back.

10. CONVOY TO SIKAR

The war frigate was as intimidating as its captain, the Master of the Guard, Minnion. As Montserrat's ship came around to its docking port, Montserrat could see the multiple artillery weapons and shielding reflectors of the frigate. This frigate was a killing machine, and it put a sour taste in the Prince's mouth.

"By the hand of Zaruhi, look at that thing!" Krueck proclaimed in amazement. "Have you ever seen such a machine?" his friend asked as he gazed out the window to see the whole spectacle.

Montserrat strapped on his weapons belt and his body shield wishing he'd been left alone on Earth and oblivious to any of this planetary bloodshed. As he glanced out the window almost dropping his weapon, he read on the side of the warship its name: *The Peacemaker*. When Montserrat was a child, his hero—his father he thought with a frown—was known as "The Peacemaker." His father had also been the captain of this battleship, once aptly named for keeping peace. Now the Prince saw it as the "Killing Ship," and he was beginning to dislike this situation even more.

As they approached the port opening, they were both met by a squad of Trans. "We are your detail team, my Prince. We are here to take you to the war room." a Trans leader explained as the guards fell into ready formation.

Being the last to exit their own ship, Krueck had activated the environmental controls on their freighter and lowered the temperature to 0 degrees. If disloyal Trans had been left on the ship, they would vacate it quickly. The Trans could not withstand the cold, and they would never be able to change a control without the authorization codes. Krueck and Montserrat always used this method of temperature control to ensure their privacy from the Trans, even since they'd been children.

"Take me to Minnion!" Montserrat ordered the guards as he and Krueck began walking down the corridor of *The Peacemaker*.

The Trans bowed, turned, and proceeded on their course. As they made their way to the conference room, Krueck telepathically put Montserrat on alert. "My Prince, did you notice his eyes when you gave him that order? They were almost transparent. He was obviously put on the defensive, but why?" Just when they neared the doorway of the War Room, Krueck perceived their danger, crying cerebrally "My Prince, something is not right here!" As they entered, Montserrat could see Minnion sitting at the conference table across the room, but to his alarm the whole room was filled with guards, so barely any space was left in the room as the Prince and Krueck entered.

Minnion stood and gave the Imperial salute but with very little attempt in showing any respect. "Montserrat, your father asked me to brief you with our mission to the Planet Sikar, the training planet for the Darrn," he explained as he raised a clawed hand to offer a seat near him.

Then as Montserrat started to make his way, a Tran's guard stepped in front of him and pulled a seat out near where Montserrat had been standing.

"My Prince, you will need something to drink. Please sit here and I will attend to you. It will be my honor!" the guard said as he gave a slight bow then quickly dashed off to get the beverage.

Minnion began to rumble, and then cleared his throat. "Yes! Refreshments would be appropriate," he crackled loudly as he took his seat across the massive table.

Krueck sat down beside Montserrat and gave the prince a confused look. The guard returned with refreshments, set them on the table; then it remained alongside Montserrat as if its job was to watch or to protect the prince—Montserrat did not know which—but at this moment, he felt safe with this Trans warrior.

As Montserrat and Krueck drank, Minnion explained the mission. "All squadrons will ascend to the planet with *The Peacemaker* in the lead. Four frigates will advance on both sides and the order will be yours to command, Montserrat."

As Minnion went over the Sikar battle tactics aloud, Krueck and Montserrat were discussing a different kind of plan between themselves telepathically. Montserrat had been assessing the war room itself and mentally backtracking the way they'd entered for a quick escape if necessary. Montserrat and Krueck knew something was awry, for the whole protocol for their briefing was unorthodox and far too many guards were present. Then as the Prince looked around the room, he noticed a data file Minnion was reading in front of him through the reflection of the mirror behind him. It was blank! Alerted, Montserrat now knew for certain he was in danger, but he would have to wait out this charade.

"Montserrat…my Prince," Minnion growled louder for Montserrat's attention. "Are you aware of the workings on this ship?"

"Yes, I'm familiar with this class warship, but I've never seen the artillery ports so intensified," Montserrat replied.

Minnion's low rumble turned into a wheezing crackle-cough as the Master of the Guard laughed. "This is the battle frigate of the warrior Valnass! He used it for mass destruction over his enemies. I have kept it as a reminder of how Valnass was a true barbarian, adding a few extra touches of my own!" As Minnion said this, he stood up and gave another faint salute to the Prince. "I will lead your flanking frigates when you give the order to attack," he concluded. The Master of the Guard then closed the data file and walked out, followed by a majority of the guards.

Rising from their seats, Montserrat turned to Krueck and said aloud, "Go back to the ship and retrieve our things. I wish to review these tactics again." Montserrat sat down again and pretended to silently look over the papers in front of him. But to his mind-reading and trustful friend, he transmitted, "Krueck, ready the freighter; I'll follow shortly. We need to get away from this convoy as quickly as possible."

Krueck gave a single nod and then walked back the way he had come. To Montserrat's surprise, the guards did not move or follow Krueck when he left.

11. THE MISSION

Krueck walked quickly but cautiously as he made his way to the Prince's freighter. He was only in the ship for a few minutes, but it was long enough to make his teeth chatter. Krueck was certain his security trick had worked. After he was sure he had not been followed, he once again activated the environmental controls to the freighter. As he set the temperature to normal, Krueck next sealed all open doors with alarms. If anyone was to attempt an unwelcome entry, Krueck would be ready. He had secured the bridge and readied the ship's defense and weapons console, so he began to do a chamber-to-chamber sweep of the ship when he noticed a door that had been previously concealed. With further investigation, Krueck noticed it was electronically locked.

Krueck, having studied artificial engineering technologies and logistics in the Academy of Nobles, made short work of disarming the system and securing the door. The smell had begun to assault his senses even before he had opened the door, but he was overwhelmed with nausea when the portal finally opened. He first looked around the room as he came to the reality of what this room had been used for, and while he walked, he sensed something mentally before he could see it—he was in the room where the Queen was held captive and abused. He surveyed the compartment with revulsion but couldn't take the smell any longer. Krueck left the room quickly to catch his breath. Then after a few minutes, he returned to seal the door when he lost his footing on something strewn on the floor and had to catch himself before he fell over a bulky chair.

When Krueck looked closer, he was astonished to see it was a cloak on the floor. It was completely clean and in spite of abhorrent odor of the rest of the room, the cloak had a pleasant smell to it that was familiar. He knew from the clothing's condition and the room's state, this item in *this* room was a new addition since the ship's takeover from the Darrn. Just as Krueck was coming to the realization of whose cloak it was, he turned in alarm to a noise behind him.

He had just whirled around with his blaster pointed in the direction of the noise, when he saw it. Krueck realized immediately he was lucky; if he hadn't set the environmental controls, he would not have had a chance to defend himself in the event of an ambush. The Trans was a milky alabaster white, and his eyes were almost as dark as onyx. "The guard must have stayed behind to surprise the Prince and me," thought Krueck.

When he moved closer for a better position to attack, Krueck noticed the Trans was moving very slowly. As if the Trans were alarmed or in pain, it lifted its clenched hand slowly appearing to raise a weapon, but to Krueck's surprise, the dying guard was unarmed and instead handed him a communication jewel. The jewel was a prism of collected information recorded for the receiver only, and the data it held would be lost if tampered with by anyone else. The guard winced at another wave of pain and said in a low, rundown voice, "The...Prince." With that, it collapsed to the floor. Krueck looked at the fallen guard's face, bent down, and then took the jewel.

Montserrat waited until he believed Krueck had had enough time to succeed in making it back to the freighter. Then he stood up and made his way into the bridge of *The Peacemaker* pretending to be checking the console and becoming more familiar with it. Walking through the bridge entrance, he gave the operator a brief salute followed by a dismissal of duty. He then explained to the crew of the bridge they needed to make ready to embark for Sikar, when a messenger came in from the Emperor. Accepting the message, he opened it quickly and read it to himself as the guard waited.

Son,

I've sent you to this sector to lead the force against the Planet of Sikar. It is the training ground for our enemy's forces. This attack will be a response to the abduction and loss of your mother. I've sent the coordinates for your journey, and to ensure you have the proper support, I've also commanded the Trans to assist your attack on our mortal enemy. As you lead this attack, remember the pain and suffering your mother, Queen Aleon, endured as well as the many others as a result of the Darrn's despicable act of treason.

God speed you on your destination,
Your father, the Emperor

The note was not signed by his father's hand, and Montserrat also noticed that the hologram was not preserved by the royal seal. He did not mention this to the Trans, but he acknowledged the acceptance of this message and sent the messenger away.

12. ESCAPE TO CHAZEN

As the ships approached the Planet of Sikar, the squadron led by Minnion flanked the lead ship, *The Peacemaker*. The freighter Krueck was piloting was ordered to move back among the accompanying ships behind the armada. As the Emperor's ships readied their weapons, multiple ships from Sikar launched a defense attack on the Imperial fleet, yet Sikar's projectile weapons had little effect on *The Peacemaker's* hull. Instead, the lead ship moved ahead and shot a volley of pulsar torpedoes that ripped through the Sikar's cyber-defense as if they were made of papier-mâché. As the prince's friend moved their freighter to the rear of the formation as ordered, the sight of the flotilla was like that of a swarm of insects. The Imperial fleet's charge seemed to be turning into chaos.

He turned to get a better view of the attack, but to his surprise Krueck saw one of the closer flanking Imperial ships blast a section of *The Peacemaker's* aft sector. Then another Imperial ship on the port side blasted the lead ship's propulsion sector. He was frozen with astonishment as he realized most of the firing ships on the Emperor's side were periodically directing their artillery at *The Peacemaker*. Krueck was setting a course to move further back when a volley of fire tore through the freighter causing it to spiral away from the Imperial armada. Then as Krueck tried to gain control, he saw *The Peacemaker* veering away in a flamed decent toward Sikar. Suddenly it erupted into a fiery ball of molten steel, and the enormous ball of flame illuminated the bridge with light and heat.

Jolted into action, Krueck started to adjust the control panel for an escape route when the Prince ran in from a nearby doorway which led to the bridge. Montserrat had secretly transferred from *The Peacemaker* back to the freighter by stowing away in the supply transport when the crew had loaded the freighter with needed supplies. He had then remained hidden away from any communication screens aboard the ship until he felt it was necessary to resume command. Before he had jumped ship, Montserrat had set the control panel on *The Peacemaker* to defend itself from enemy ships, and then he'd set the warship's automated co-pilot to fly into the fight. After he had eluded the guards on the bridge, Montserrat made his way to the ship's supply transport silos. Now, Montserrat was glad he had listened to Krueck. He and Krueck felt certain they had walked into an ambush, so they devised a plan of escape. With the destruction of *The Peacemaker*, they nodded to each other in confirmation that they were right.

Montserrat took control of the ship again, and they began to make the rest of their pre-planned escape. They felt another jolt as the freighter was struck again with hostile fire. The Prince began adjusting the ship's armor when the freighter was hit so hard that both pilots toppled against the console panel and crashed to the floor. Aftershocks of electrical explosions and sparks erupted everywhere, filling the bridge with ion smoke, and after a time, the freighter's bridge shut down completely, now crippled and defenseless.

The attack halted and as Montserrat and Krueck both regained their bearings, they simultaneously thought the same idea: they were about to be boarded! They scrambled to the nearby armory and grabbed as many weapons as the two could carry. If the freighter was going to be attacked, they were not going down without a fight. Krueck's lacerated head was bleeding, but he was well enough to continue the fight.

Montserrat suddenly had a cunning idea that would take the enemy by surprise, and Krueck would be the decoy. He then stationed himself along the only corridor the attackers would be able to come down, and he sat still for awhile, but it seemed nothing was happening. The corridor was dark and all Montserrat could see was the periodic sparks from the electrical conduits damaged from the initial blasts, and he would certainly have missed the transparent attackers if he wasn't suddenly telepathically warned by Krueck.

The assassins stepped over Krueck who was sprawled on the floor in the corridor pretending to be dead. To Krueck's shock, the attackers were Trans! The Prince could barely make out the translucent eyes as they walked over Krueck's body in the hallway. Montserrat set his projectile weapon on the would-be assassins when he noticed their blue eyes were staring right at him. He couldn't believe his father's guards were attacking *him* and his ship's crew! To Montserrat's advantage, the Trans had not known he was aboard until they spotted him in this hold out. But why hadn't they ceased` their attack when they noticed him? They were supposed to protect the Royal family at all costs.

"*Just come a little bit further,*" he thought, as he braced himself for the fight, and held his fire.

The Trans defectors stepping over Krueck had not realized he was still alive. Then just at the very moment before the Trans could get an advantage, Krueck sat up, as he and Montserrat fired on the assassins. The Trans were fast— although not fast enough to repel their attackers. The two men continued until the last Trans had expired.

As the two young men made their way back to the command bridge, Krueck explained to the prince what he had observed earlier during the battle. He was furious about the treachery of the Trans, but Krueck was confused about something else and asked his prince to follow him to the infirmary instead. Within seconds, Montserrat saw why Krueck had headed there.

A Trans was on a life support pack. Krueck explained as he checked on the progress of the support system how he'd received a communication jewel (breaking from Imperial protocol) from this Trans. While handing over the jewel communicator and as the Trans smiled up at Montserrat, Krueck explained that the guard had risked its life to get the jewel and its data into the prince's hands by staying behind on their frigid freighter. In a split second as Montserrat noticed the Trans' relief, Krueck saw the translucent face abruptly transform into a scowl. Suddenly, the Trans lunged off of the gurney and landed in front of Krueck and Montserrat.

A blast flashed in the room, and the young men turned to see two more conspiring Trans attackers followed by a Minrall, rush in and blast the faithful Trans across the table to the floor. With no way to escape, Montserrat and Krueck were now trapped by the three invaders. The Minrall, who seemed younger than the one Montserrat encountered back on Earth, started to rumble a laugh that turned into a grumbling gurgle as it shape-shifted into the Master of the Guard.

"Hello my Prince," the Minrall laughed as he shuffled into the room behind the defecting Trans, who were now aiming weapons at the two captives. "You're as slippery as a Phirra serpent," the shape shifter exclaimed as it shifted back to its original Minrall form. "You were so easy to lure here, and now I get to kill you myself. I will take this as an immense honor to be the one who mounts your head on my hall. After this, I will have the respect deserving to my clan. However, you will not feel agony if you die too quickly; instead I will take you back to my hall and teach you the true meaning of pain," choked the Minrall as he stepped back.

The Minrall then signaled to the attacking Trans, and they advanced toward their captives. One of the Trans handed Montserrat a restraint shackle and was ordering Krueck to grab the other end, when suddenly the disloyal Trans' face erupted into a flash of opalescent matter and collapsed. More flashing and noise screamed as the second two-faced Trans became another victim of gunfire. Finding itself now unshielded the Minrall advanced on the Prince. Weapon held high, the faithful Trans messenger jumped from behind the table and entwined its arms and legs around the hulking beast. It stabbed the Minrall in the neck with a flash-knife and was about to sheer off the lump of a head in a victorious attempt when its strength gave way from its injuries. The Minrall quickly overpowered the weakened Trans and ended the fight with a shattering blow to the head of the Trans still barely clinging to the upper torso of the beast.

The Trans fell from the Minrall like a sack of rocks. This struggle, however, was enough of a distraction for a shadowy figure in the hall to blast off the humongous right leg of the Minrall, just as it had turned to exact revenge on the Prince. To Montserrat's disbelief, the real Master of the Guard, bloody and mangled, limped into the room. Growling with a hideous look, face shaking, eyes in a berserk state, and then giving up to its own fatigue, Minnion collapsed with a loud crunching thud. Krueck swiftly lifted his weapon and trained it on the Minrall; the Prince then fastened a neutralizing restraint to the Minrall stopping the creature from shape-shifting or moving without excruciating and paralyzing pain to its cerebral cortex.

After securing the wounded true Master of the Guard to their freighter's sickbay and transporting the Minrall prisoner to a stasis cell, Montserrat was able to chart an escape to the nearest planetary sector. While Krueck plotted the course, the Prince stared at his friend for what seemed a millennium. The Prince finally turned toward the console with a look of distress.

Krueck, placing a hand on the shoulder of his Prince said, "We have no other choice my friend," and standing silently by Montserrat, he then headed the ship to the Chazen Sector.

13. GIRON GOJII

After landing the freighter and boarding a waiting ferry, Montserrat thought back to the first time he was on the planet Giro. Montserrat was just as taken then as he was now sailing across the sea to the Palace of Ganaka because it was in many ways, breathtaking. Even the ship the prince was now sailing on reminded him of the vessels on Earth called 'junkets' made from bamboo and pine which he'd studied when he'd lived in Japan. Montserrat was the most comfortable in Asia as it was so close to the Giron's culture. He'd only left Asia because it became unbearable to stay there without thinking of Gojii or imagining he was seeing her around every corner.

The ship lunged forward as the current shifted slightly. Montserrat held on and looked toward the jungle's shore. As he approached, he recognized the top spires and the multiple rooftops of the Palace which were sticking out of the tops of the foliage. The Palace shone as bright as gold from the reflection of the suns in the Chazen sector.

A flock of scaled seabirds, the favorite food of Pedfish, burst out from the water as the ship trekked further. The seabirds were bright orange with white patches. Their scales reflected like lustrous pearls as they clung tightly against the body of these lean seabirds, and their wings resembled beautiful webs as they fluttered in the misty air. The seabirds abruptly broke to the right, following the lead creature as it plunged headfirst back into the depths of the sea. Montserrat felt the ship's speed slow a little as the vessel began to reach the shore; upon moving closer to the edge of the shore, the ship halted and began to rise out of the water.

The junket was strapped to the enormous reddish-green, tortoise-skinned body of a Giant Pedfish as it came out of the water and began to walk toward the towering land pier. The maw of the huge fish dripped with the remains of some of the seabirds which were not fast enough to avoid it. The vessel on top of the Pedfish shifted from side to side as the sea creature's giant legs slogged toward the pagoda-style pier. Upon reaching its destination, the Pedfish knelt down beside the pier and began to chew on the few remaining seabirds captured in its large baleen. It stretched out to get comfortable while digesting its food and to catch some of the sun's excellence.

As the ship also settled in beside the pier, the attendants from the dock ran up to the deck and tied the junket down by its cleats. The port official recognized Prince Montserrat and bowed deeply.

"My Lord, it honors us to have you here on Giro," the official said as he grinned broadly and rose from his profound bow.

The Prince called to Krueck and turned to watch the pier attendants walking up with his friend along with the gurney holding Minnion. Montserrat then heard a loud disturbance and looked below to see the Giron's dragging the thwarted Minrall as the hulking rock complained—to no avail—on its treatment. Though every counter movement caused it more pain, the Minrall kept trying to grab the prison walls as it was brought closer to its holding cell.

Meanwhile, the Girons who escorted the Minrall pierced the creature with a barbed spike, and as each barb made contact, it dissolved the beast's tissue. Much like a sandblaster erodes rock; the tissue then fell to the ground like a torn bag of sand. This was a most effective punishment because the Minrall gradually stopped fighting and began to walk in defeatism toward its cell's platform.

Montserrat addressed a few more Giron security orders with the official before he and Krueck began their ascent on a palanquin-like transporter to the entrance of the Palace. As they approached the front gate, women clad in billowing gowns converged in a long line on the transport. The gowns' fabric was so fine that it appeared weightless in the cool breeze coming up from the sea. Each woman was dressed in a different color, with a face more beautiful than her successor. As the group arrived at the entrance, the women began pining for the visitors' attention.

Krueck looked toward Montserrat with a mischievous smile. "*Why* did we ever decide to leave this planet again?" he asked as he eagerly began to step down from the platform.

"I'm sure it will come to you eventually," Montserrat replied while he followed the lead of the port official.

Suddenly, a woman adorned in a bright silver gown and sparkling jewels stepped out from behind a buggy. She raised her hand and exclaimed vehement insults to the other women and waved them away with a single gesture. The fearful women fled in every direction pushing Krueck out of the way as if the angry woman was about to lethally explode if they remained or disobeyed.

Montserrat saw the angered woman, and he knew immediately it was Gojii. Emotions flooded over him with just the sight of her. Showing herself to be very athletic, she made short work of the distance between her and the fleeing women. Her silken dress was a beautiful fashion which accentuated her amazing figure. Her long black locks of hair flowed loosely with her elegant studded hairpins keeping her picturesque face and emerald eyes clear. Her sumptuous red lips were painted to perfection, and as Gojii spoke her native tongue to her subordinates, Montserrat was mesmerized once again by the woman he loved. No time or distance made a difference to his feelings for Gojii—she was the most beautiful woman on the Planet Giro.

Her superior beauty was a fact in reality because a Giron edict stated that its highest honor was only awarded to the most beautiful and gifted woman on Giro. Gojii was the daughter of the highly notorious woman, Namiko, known historically to all Girons. Namiko, a warrior general of the Giron sisterhood, was said to be very ruthless. It was said Gojii's father was a rivaling noble of this sector; he and Namiko were married as an arrangement so civil battles would end. Montserrat had seen her several times when he'd been on this planet years earlier, and yes, Namiko was beautiful indeed.

When Montserrat was older, he almost fell for Namiko's ways of persuasion until Gojii came into his life and saved him from her mother's clutches. When Gojii was little, she was fun and full of questions because she was very interested in the royal life of her new friend. They were both young, so they were left to play and frolic together as the adults completed their business affairs. Montserrat and Gojii's past adventures included many sea voyages and sea-star hunting.

It was during one adventure that Montserrat remembered the first time they had kissed on the shore of the palace's reef—years had passed and many meetings had occurred. Later they became lovers, and though Montserrat was warned about the trickery of the women from this kingdom, he wouldn't listen to the well-advised rumors of his peers. Montserrat *knew* his woman; Gojii was very devoted to him, and their love *was* genuine.

Finally, Montserrat denounced the warnings from his advisors as well as his father's insistence and constant reminders of the Darr law. Then in the year when the water turned black and a huge flood devastated Giro, Montserrat left his duties at home and flew back to the planet to make sure Gojii was safe. Gojii's parents had remained on the planet to help evacuate the villagers from eminent danger, but everyone left behind perished. Montserrat spent months consoling Gojii on the loss of her father and mother. It was later learned the flood was caused by the Darrn. They were attempting to start an Imperial war which failed under the tremendous hand of the Emperor's Imperial army. Montserrat learned of a Giron betrayal which had caused great hardship to his father's army and to the Giron people; eventually, the leak was traced back and blamed on the Giron house.

All evidence pointed to Gojii's family, but there was never any conviction by the Emperor after the deaths of Gojii's parents. The Emperor felt the loss was enough of a punishment to Gojii, but this lesser judgment was also due to pleads from Montserrat on her behalf. Therefore, Montserrat was commanded to never return to this sector and to cut all ties. The problem, however, was Montserrat was never given the chance to explain or say goodbye to Gojii. He had thought back to this time as he caught sight of her now, moving to the stairwell. Gojii twisted her head to look down upon him. Her long hair fell gently across her bare shoulder as she now looked at Montserrat with expressed contempt.

Gojii turned abruptly and walked upward and through the palace gates. Montserrat wanted to follow after her, but the prince was trapped by the attending diplomats and his royal obligations. This protocol was the part Prince Montserrat disliked and hadn't missed during his absence from Darr.

As Montserrat began to go up the stairs, he saw Krueck.

"K, stay close, we have many things we need to go over," Montserrat said mentally to his friend. "I'll need you in one hour. Then we'll both interrogate that shape-shifting rock!" he ardently continued as he walked in the other direction of Krueck.

"Yes, my prince. But I can come now if you need me," Krueck responded pulling away from the women as he noticed Montserrat's brief encounter with Gojii had disturbed his friend.

"No!" Montserrat interrupted almost brusquely, and waved Krueck away. "Go have some fun. I'll be fine."

After making his arrangements with the palace, changing into more comfortable attire, and making his greeting known throughout, an hour later Montserrat made his way to the holding pen. Krueck was late, and the Prince hoped his friend was on his way. The prison's most secure holding pen was a vast hole carved from solid steel. It was electrically charged with water from a high voltage conductor; this hole was used for interrogation of Minralls. If the probe was successful, it wouldn't be long before the shape-shifter would give up the name of its accomplice. If it was not a success, much of the Minrall's body would be converted to sand or glass depending on how hot the probes' sensors became. As the prince approached the pen, he was not surprised at what he heard.

"You won't get a confession from me!" the captive snarled through clenched teeth that looked like stained marbles. "I am from the Clan of Minrall. We cannot be broken by mere pain!"

The floor was already speckled with glass beads and sporadic sand piles before Krueck quickly returned to his friend's side. Montserrat, standing there with his arms crossed, glared down through the domed shield at his prisoner. He had learned of the Minrall's attempt on his life, but it still had not confessed the name of its co-conspirator. It admitted to taking *The Peacemaker* by force as a shape-shift of the Master of the Guard.

The Minrall had even executed the torture of Minnion and had left him for dead on the shuttle floor. As the interrogation continued, the Minrall cursed the fact that it hadn't squeezed the last breath from the half-breed before it had left to meet with the Prince. The prisoner squealed as the probe dug deeper into its triceps and leg joints.

Montserrat began to explain to Krueck in the Minrall's hearing that the Minrall had even deceived the Trans to believing it was the Master of the Guards. The Minrall then had called for the meeting in the war room so it could be close enough to strike. If it hadn't been for the protection of some unconvinced Trans, the shape-shifter's plan would have worked, and it could have gotten close enough to kill the prince. The Minrall was disappointed that the faithful Trans were more numerous than the defectors, and the Minrall knew when it had been found out by the Trans guards. Montserrat cut short his report to Krueck when he noticed the Minrall's ranting was about to give them a confirmation. Montserrat held his finger up to his mouth and pointed to let Krueck listen.

"It all was to look like an accident and then we were to report back to his-"

Just then, the Minrall was able to release its bound arm, and it grabbed the probe. The probe had a defense mechanism to prevent such a breach, and it lit up as though it was overloading. As the Minrall held on to the electrode, it squealed louder as the pain overtook the Minrall's senses. In a flash, the room was atomized with spays of flying sand and glass. But before Montserrat could get everything shut down, what little there was of the Minrall left, could not be defined as a living object any longer. Montserrat ordered the room to be cleaned and walked into an adjacent room with Krueck.

As the high-powered vents began to make short work of the clean up, the doors closed so the two could have privacy and talk. When some Giron

women came into the room to serve some refreshments, the two friends'
conversation reverted back to mental communication.

Montserrat started by asking Krueck, "Who do you think the Minrall
was referring to when it said, "Report back to his…"

One of the ladies stopped to rub Krueck's neck, but Montserrat stood
and dismissed her abruptly, then with a continuing stern tone of authority
in Giro, he ordered the room not to be disturbed. With the other women
leading the way out, she turned and closed the door quickly behind her.

"This has been a stressful day for you, Montserrat. Why don't you take
a rest?" Krueck suggested as he poured his friend a drink. "I'll check on
Minnion to see if he's now conscious." Concurring, Montserrat dropped
back into his seat and accepted the offered cup.

"I am tired," he said sipping the warm drink.

It was soothing to him to have some Giron Ale again. The fermented
nectar of the exotic seabirds was a delicacy throughout the kingdom, and
like he remembered, it was warm and full-bodied. If he had to compare it to
anything—which is what he had been doing a great deal of since he had
returned—it was much like the Terra drink he'd often enjoyed and what
humans called malt whiskey. The only difference here on Giro was the fact
that this drink was warmed over a fire to intensify its strength and flavor,
though this glass of Giron Ale had an aftertaste he did not recall. He
suddenly looked at the glass, and he knew the danger before he heard the
sound of Krueck fall from his chair. They had been drugged!

Montserrat woke up to the smell of flowers and the haze of the
incense burning in the room. Looking around, he could see the elaborate
and colorful hangings draped over the dark carvings and walls of the
chamber. Rare plants and trees were moving by the soft breeze that was
filtered in from an unknown source. He was on a bed fabricated of the
softest urchin silk, decorated with a mass of tassels and braids framing the

bedding. Realizing the soft silk was against his naked body, he sat up slowly from his bed and rubbed his head. He looked down one of the long archways of the room to see tubs of scented pedals; the pools were elegantly surrounded by hundreds of lighted candles. Gold embellished trinkets were strewn throughout the room and a dozen sculptures were sitting in niches watching over his location, much like spiritual guardians.

Montserrat realized he'd been there for some time when he noticed the sun was rising. He turned toward the right archway to see a shimmering curtain. Behind the curtain stood a silhouette of a woman; she was completely naked. He could see the curving small of her back and the firm roundness of her breasts as she shifted her weight to her left. Her arms lifted an elegant robe over her buttocks, and then she wrapped it around herself. She pulled her hair from the back of her collar, and let it fall over her like a shawl.

She stepped lightly down off of the platform and passed the curtain with the slightest of effort. Her sultry movements stirred Montserrat's insides as he got out of bed, and met up with her. He grabbed her hand gently and turned her toward him. She smiled softly and leaned forward and gave him a soft but luring kiss.

"Good morning, my love. You are awake?" she whispered cajolingly to him with her eyes still closed as she took in the moment. Gojii was always so happy and welcoming to Montserrat. He touched her chin, and she opened her eyes to meet his gaze. "What shall we do today?" she asked rubbing his muscular arm while he wrapped it around her waist.

He stared at her and took another glance at the pools of flowered water. "We could take another bath, if you'd like?" he asked as he pressed himself against her.

"We took a bath last evening," she said while trying to squirm away from his arms. "Besides, the water is cold—and I would have to get it heated again!" she said laughing as he pulled her closer by her robe's knot. He lifted her into his arms and turned toward the bed.

The door to her chamber chimed, and he set her down on the bed. He looked for his robe, and spotted it in a corner by the nearest tub.

"What is it?" he called out while dressing.

"My prince, your father has summoned you," the Giron guard stated through the door.

Montserrat looked at his woman, and gave her a surprised shrug. "So much for another bath," he sighed to her quietly.

"I'll be along shortly. Ready my transport!" he called out to the waiting guard. Then he turned back toward the bed.

Gojii wasn't there. He turned to find her, and she had already begun dressing in her riding gear. "Hey what are you doing?" Montserrat asked as if he was hurt.

"I have to get back to my duties," Gojii said as she pulled up her boots. "I can't stay in bed forever! I have something else to do now that you're summoned away."

She stood up and gave him a piercing look. "Are you coming back, or should I find something else to do tonight?" she asked as she fixed his robe.

He grabbed her again and said quietly in her ear, "I will be back for another bath." He gave her a gentle kiss and held her close.

"I'll get it hot for you my love," she said back, and ran off laughing, she had pulled off his robe, and he was standing there naked when the door flung open to a crowded courtyard.

Jolted from his dream, Montserrat awoke with a blinding headache. He was not in the room of his memory, but in a stateroom of a rapidly moving sea sloop on the Sea of Giro. The sound of orders was being relayed to the crew, and Montserrat could hear people running on deck above. As he looked around, Montserrat was a little shaky as he lifted himself off the bed.

The prince took in his surroundings, and noticed Minnion strapped on a stasis gurney.

Montserrat tried to summon Krueck, only to realize his friend was not around. Montserrat then looked for a weapon, but found none. The seal to the room opened, and Gojii walked in with a tray. She looked at him briefly while setting it down then bent down and checked the sensors to Minnion's gurney.

Everything looking acceptable, she walked up to Montserrat, and slapped his face. She stared at him for some time, and then fell into his arms. He held her tight and caressed Gojii caringly, who was now sobbing.

"Giron women never cry," Montserrat thought. They are conditioned at an early age to never express emotions because to show emotion in public was a sign of weakness. Montserrat held her even tighter, as her weeping subsided.

"We will reach the emergency lift shortly; I thought you might want something to eat," she quietly said. Gojii then began to walk away, but Montserrat caught her by the arm. "We have a lot to talk about," he said as he moved toward her. She turned abruptly and faced him.

"What is going on here? And why have your Trans guards suddenly begun attacking the city?" Gojii asked curtly. "I think they are after you Montserrat!" "We were only able to get to this ship by luck," Gojii continued to explain to Montserrat as she pushed on the compartment over the headboard and it sprung open. They both grabbed the hidden lash guns and blades. They were interrupted by an immense explosion which had erupted somewhere outside.

"I thought we had more time, but I was wrong!" Gojii exclaimed as they both strapped on their shields.

"Where is Krueck?" Montserrat asked as he quickly followed her up to the deck.

"He went ahead to ready the ship."

To his surprise, the seas were filled with fleeing runners in every direction. Montserrat watched in shock; the Palace was in flames as the attacking fleet bombarded it with projectile missiles. The largest tower began to fall in a horrific crash as flames billowed upward and debris flew everywhere. Many ships were turning toward the sea. As the sloop began to turn into the platform lift, they were hit by a shower of water as the blasts grew closer.

Just as the shield came up, an inferno of fire caused another explosion, blowing apart the dock entrance. Surprisingly, the sloop locked into the lift and shot upwards toward the freighter before the flames engulfed the entire dock below.

14. BETRAYAL

Sitting on his throne, the Emperor nervously fiddled with his robes as the Darrn walked into the assembly room. The Emperor abruptly stopped what he was doing and sat straight up. He reminded himself to stay calm and unreadable as the members of the Darrn's procession entered and gradually took their places. The Emperor had ordered the Trans to double the guards during the day's sessions because he was uneasy with the proceedings involving the Battle of Supremacy. Once the Cyclo Arena was readied by other officials, the treaty could then be set between the Emperor and the Chancellor of Darrn.

The Chancellor walked over to the Podium, and it leered at the Emperor, snickered slightly, and then shifted its gaze around the room at the overwhelming audience and the many nearly-invisible Trans.

With a crash of the gavel, the Chancellor cleared its throat with a grinding gurgle. "By the laws of Darr and the Rule of Nobility, the Clan demands the Emperor announce the champion to fight in the Cyclo Arena," it declared. "It is by law that the rite must be observed by both factions, and if the Emperor cannot announce his champion, perhaps he would like to defend the throne personally?" it asked turning its large body toward the host while gripping the podium.

The Emperor observing how this caused a stir among the court, was very unhappy with this unusual opening tactic. Still, he remained coolheaded as he remembered his conversation with his son a few years earlier.

"The heir to the throne must compete to hold our place at the kingdom's Gate. Without this contest, we will lose all of the holdings and the victor can claim its place on the throne and banish mankind for the decades of five," the Emperor had said from the throne, frowning at Montserrat. Then more sternly, he added, "Why can't you participate?"

"Valnass protected *your* throne. Why can't we have someone else contend for mine?" Montserrat had questioned.

"Valnass was my best friend and like a brother to me. Because of my health and the love your grandfather had for him, he was permitted to take my place. The Great Darrn thought it would be victorious over Valnass because Valnass was unknown in our realm," explained the emperor to his son. "The Great Darrn was wrong—thankfully so."

Now though, the Emperor remembered in self-disgust how he'd not been forthright with Montserrat. *"The truth of the matter was that my father, the late Emperor, trusted Valnass over me because my father felt I was weak,"* he'd thought as he adjusted his posture. *"I was gutless. I should have taken care of Valnass when I found out he was my older half-brother by my father's mistress."*

Valnass had defeated the Darrn several times before the great fight on Cyclo mount. *"He had the rite to be the true heir to the throne at that time. But to my great fortune, the filthy treacherous Darrn had used a tainted and barbed blade in the arena, and though Valnass had defeated the Great Darrn, the poison from the Darrn's barbs took Valnass' life a few days later. His win assured me of the victory for the next Decades of Five,"* he thought.

His attention returned to the present, hiding his shame, the Emperor lowered his head as he responded to the Darrn's challenge. "I would accept the challenge of course, but I've gone to many lengths to get the "Champion of the Mount" prepared to rightfully defend our throne."

"The throne!" The Chancellor barked as if he was spewing a mouth full of venom. "You must *win* the throne before it is yours! We have executed a Backtar! Therefore, *you* must have your champion here before the third full-moon sets or you *forfeit* your holdings!" it roared as it began to move back to its seat.

The Emperor jumped to his feet and with contempt for the Darrn's manner he sharply said, "I would advise you to prepare yourselves as you did before. It's only then that you'll *ever* see the throne for yourselves. Now get out!"

With this, the Chancellor of Darrn grabbed his staff and walked out of the throne room calmly with a slight grin on his face.

Returning again to his thoughts of the past the Emperor remembered saying to Montserrat, "It took six of those beasts to take Valnass! You're our only hope, and you are Darr's champion!"

Embarrassed by his own silence, the Emperor looked around to see his chamber of officials looking at him, so he gave a quick nod, and the next chancellor of business was admitted.

The launching dock was deep within the mountain, as the sloop locked onto the platform. The groaning sounds of overhanging metal and concrete structures were giving way to the fierce bombardment, and the noise was growing. It would take a few minutes for the attacking fleet to get through the defense shield, but not much more than that. Every decision made now was vital to their survival.

As they ran down the tube toward the ship, Krueck met up with them both. "Montserrat, we need to go this way!" he cried as he pushed them left. Then as they started to run up an exhaust shaft, they heard the ship blast off from the dock.

Krueck saw a flash of light, and shoved Montserrat and Gojii into a service alcove. He snapped on his shield, and as they fell into the door jam, Krueck braced himself against the small opening. Krueck looked as if he was being pulled in different directions as he gripped the door jam. Grimacing and struggling to hold his ground, he kicked back and held on even tighter as though he was being tugged back. When Montserrat rolled over to see his friend's struggle, the face of a Trans appeared. Montserrat then realized who was pulling on Krueck to get inside. Suddenly, the exhaust from the ship's burners ripped through the shaft, snatching the Trans from Krueck's back, and almost taking Krueck with it.

He'd deflected the flame as a human door, but the flame had expelled almost all of its heat just beyond Krueck. Montserrat had shielded Gojii as the flash of the burners' eruption engulfed his line of sight. Krueck had grunted in agony as the blast hit his shield and armor while igniting the shaft. When the flames went out, Krueck fell into the hole with Montserrat and Gojii.

Krueck, blistered slightly, and battered, still remained low then moved closer to the door to see if anyone else was in pursuit.

Looking back to Montserrat, he said "We need to get back to the sloop," then turned again to the door again to watch for any sign of another attack. "I talked too much to one of my lady friends, and she sold us out!" he added as he gingerly stood up. "I took care of her, though. She was on that ship, as . . . a guest. I said we'd take her for a ride when we left, and they were just waiting for us!

The snake was on that ship, and I'm sure she'll have some explaining to do!" Krueck grunted smugly.

Krueck needed help walking, so the two assisted him back to the sloop. The sloop was still intact, but it had sustained some exterior damage.

The Prince hit the entry code, and the door swung open leading to the galley where Gojii could care for Krueck's wounds.

Before Montserrat stepped through the doorway to go back on deck, Krueck grabbed his arm, "I'm sorry my Prince, you told me to be careful."

Montserrat looked at him and gave him a grin. "Now, do you remember why we left this planet?" he looked at Gojii, turned, and left as she began administering to Krueck.

He waited for awhile then slowly disengaged the sloop from the platform and emerged from the dock.

"The Trans weren't looking for prisoners," Montserrat mentally concluded as he saw the remains of his freighter smoldering on the side of the beach.

He checked the sensors around the area and set his course in the opposite direction of the fleet's exhaust signature. They were going to need a better means of escape, he thought to himself. Gojii and Krueck had stepped on deck and were viewing the wreckage as Montserrat circled the sloop around to the north.

"We need to find another transport," Montserrat said as he made room for Krueck and Gojii.

"We can go to the farm. We have a harvest shipyard there," Gojii replied. Gojii grabbed the gears and Montserrat let her take over.

"We don't have a defense if they come back. Is there a weapons port there?" he asked.

"Yes," she replied. Gojii was putting the ship into a rapid dive when she handed him a communication jewel. "Krueck gave this to me before we separated in the palace," Gojii explained as she pulled up on the throttle and banked right.

Montserrat took the jewel but was somewhat upset at his friend.

"I knew it was safe," Krueck said, moving uncomfortably in his seat.

"Krueck also explained how your father ordered you to leave Giro," she continued, "and how you didn't have a chance to tell me. But it looks like you may have believed your father," she said, irritated and hurt as she pulled back the controls of the sloop for a landing at the farm's shoreline.

Looking over the vast hills of farmland, the Prince observed the rolling land with lush foliage and vegetation. From one side of the valley to the next, the land was still full of morning mist from the dense rainfall the evening before. Montserrat also observed the robotic harvesters walking through the crops swinging giant scythes, shearing through the crops with ease and perfect precision. As these robots trudged through the rows of crops, little metallic pickers buzzed around them plucking the vegetation and distributing the produce it into fishnet sacks to haul back to the silos for more sorting.

The fresh air and the low precipitous clouds hovering overhead made Montserrat feel at ease, considering the night had been filled with surprising and unwelcome information.

He turned his attention to the device given to him by Gojii. The communication jewel the faithful Trans had given Krueck contained information on Lady Dreann's whereabouts as well as the details about the conspiracy from the shape-shifter. The Trans had taken Lady Dreann from the freighter to protect her, and had left her secure under allied guards on the Island of Stamis. The island was home to a hybrid of the giant Stamen plant, known to have a poison-bearing anther. The plant was usually used as a decoration or a deterrent from intruders on private properties, but the poison from its synthesized pollen was often used by the Darrn as an illegal slow-killing elixir.

The jewel continued to report Lady Dreann would be safe from the revolt of the "traitor" as long as she stayed in the island's fortress. The Trans felt it was the easiest way to protect her, and it was in the one place the rebellious Trans wouldn't look: right under their noses. Montserrat also learned the revolt of the Trans occurred when each guard was forced to choose which power to follow. Using this new information together with what he already knew, he now remembered the events that had taken place. An evil thought came to mind. But when he dismissed it as quickly as it had come, a question remained: why did some Trans follow him and others try to destroy him? Its answer became an ongoing argument in his head: "*It couldn't be true. No, it couldn't be. Could it?*"

Then Montserrat had another idea. "*Could I be fighting, yet another faction I'm unaware of?*"

At the end of the communicator's transmission it became fuzzy and full of static; in fact, the jewel seemed interrupted at the end. Krueck had told Montserrat the interruption was from the temperature change he had set onboard the freighter before exiting the ship. The jewel attempted to generate a message of reflected memory, but as the Trans gave in to the cold, so did the jewel.

Abruptly, the transmitter hooked to Montserrat's arm beeped, "The ship is ready my Prince. Shall we be on our way?" Krueck asked. Montserrat exhaled relief as he anticipated this news for the last two weeks.

"We'll leave as soon as possible, I have something to address. Where's Gojii?" Montserrat asked bending down to pick up his belt.

Just as he did so, a loud buzzing sound ripped past his head. Montserrat fell to the floor and rolled to move out of the way. The Harvester finished climbing over the edge of the platform and began to adjust its arm for another swipe at the prince. Montserrat tried to grab for his shield-belt but suddenly jumped out of the way; the machine stepped on the belt crushing it under its padded foot.

Whirling around, Montserrat barely missed being crushed by the moving arm but it managed to clip the prince, and sent Montserrat flying into the wall planter full of flowering horned tendrils. The prince jumped forward and high, grabbing onto an overhang as the blade sliced through the planters and the large thick pillars of the veranda.

The Portico then toppled on the machine, but the robot shrugged it off as if it was a bothersome insect. Montserrat knew he couldn't keep this up much longer unless he could find a clearing. Exhausted and cut up as he was, Montserrat needed to generate enough energy to defend himself. As he made his way to the edge of the deck, another crash began and Montserrat's footing gave way, as the whole deck collapsed to the next level. Hurtling over debris, Montserrat found an opening and ran inside as fast as he could.

"It's not giving me a second to recover," Montserrat thought as he was passing a towering obsidian fountain, when it too exploded, by the force of the swinging robotic arm.

The gnarled fountain fragments knocked him to the floor. Part of the blade broke off and landed beside Montserrat's head. He grabbed it just in time as the harvester's remaining long blade sliced through the solid teak partition and knocked Montserrat through an open windowed doorway onto a smaller balcony. Montserrat barely caught himself on the metal railing before he'd have hurled over the side. Bracing himself, Montserrat saw the hulking metallic body burst through the opening of the French doors and stop.

Montserrat now saw the outline of a female figure in the machine's fogged cockpit. The pilot's black hair whipped frantically from side to side while she controlled the toggles, and manipulated the massive arm to lift up for a final strike with its blade was buzzing louder as it gained momentum once again. Dangling by his arms Montserrat was about to let go when Krueck appeared, hovering midair behind the prince in the newly repaired harvest freighter. Krueck blasted the berserk machine with precise aim using star disrupters which knocked the machine back.

As the star disrupters sizzled through the Plexiglass and found its target, the broken machine crashed back into the entry with its lifeless pilot in a cloud of smoke. Montserrat reached up toward the hatch as Krueck piloted the ship closer to the ledge. To his shock, Gojii was holding out her hand.

"Grab on, my love!" she yelled as Montserrat stared at her.

Montserrat grabbed Gojii's hand, and she pulled him into her arms. Montserrat then held her tight against him breathing a long sigh of relief.

15. THE CHALLENGE OF THE DARRN

The third moon was in its last few hours, and the brilliance of the other two orbs were now in darkness. Standing in his enormous sitting room, the Emperor stared at the last full moon with a longing feeling. As he looked down, he held in his hand a picture of the late Queen in her wedding gown. The Emperor traced his jeweled finger down the edge of her beautiful face. He drank the final crimson dregs from his goblet and without another glance, he suddenly flung it across the room, where it crashed and shattered against the carved malachite fireplace.

After a few seconds, the Emperor walked over to his dressing stand and placed the crown of supremacy on his head then clipped the sword of champions, the twin-bladed sword of his ancestors, to his sash. He then walked from his private quarters and signaled to the Trans to fall in.

"I need all of you to be alert," the Emperor said as he addressed his captain of the guards. "I expect you will have a new Emperor by the end of this spectacle," he grumbled as the great doors swung open to the crowd. "God help you . . . and curse you," he sneered as he walked out into the arena waving to the crowd with his hand cupped in a salute.

The Chancellor of Darrn then stepped out from behind the podium, and turned the antique handle signaling the arena. The enormous gong sounded with its reverberating thunder throughout the entire Cyclo arena. The ceremony had begun! Then the arena fell silent as the Emperor stepped up onto a podium opposite the Chancellor. With the push of a lever, he traditionally responded to the challenge from the Darrn. Upon the signal from the Emperor, a flock of flying Centicors was released. Hundreds of serpent-looking lizards with long winged bodies flew out in formation encircling the arena with an elegant fluidity, and sparkling with the luminance of various hypnotic-colors. The Centicors rounded the risers and abruptly scattered as they approached the entry to the arena as if sensing another presence. The festivities began with a large complement of heralding horns and drums as a group of decorated dancers ran out to the arena's center. Confetti strings and ribbon sequins fluttered from the balcony as the traditional twirling streamers and multicolored banners flew through the air directed to the dancers in the arena. The dancing and frolicking were an unbelievable spectacle, and the Emperor was impressed even as reality set in and his inevitable end drew nearer. He saw the many court officials, all the royal clans, and even the Queen's court laughing and drinking their sparkling Zorillian ale.

Then as the crowd watched, the entry of the Darrn warriors caused the celebration to take a horrific turn. In the past the Battles of Supremacy had been under greater supervision by the Master of the Guard and the Trans when the opposing clan entered the arena, but as the Darrn warriors entered the Arena today, they'd been allowed to claw their way into the grounds. Breathing heavily and with grumbling fury, they pounced with hunger as they made short work of the unsuspecting dancers. Horror struck the audience as they watched the hairy and hulking monsters clawing and chewing through the decoratively costumed dancers—and spewing saliva everywhere—once they'd finally found what they were so frenzied over: food. The Imperial guards came to the quick defense of the fleeing prey and the lower level occupants who'd been unlucky enough to get a ground level stadium seat. One of the attackers had just come upon the nearest occupied box, when the Trans swarmed the area with a flood of lash projectiles. As the long toothy mouth of the attacking Darrn came down on its victim, the Darrn's head was blown apart and the body slumped to the ground. Loud tinny warnings were being growled toward the other advancing beasts as the Trans' reinforcements arrived and started to retaliate. Now staring at the Trans, the remaining Darrns retreated from the mass of guards, grunted then cleaned their claws as they licked the bloody remains of the dancers from themselves.

The Emperor stood solemn as he watched the Chancellor from across the arena. The Chancellor then caught the ruler looking at him, and turned toward the Emperor and glared at him with a fanged grin. As the Chancellor began his ritual challenge, the Emperor could now feel the elixir he had added to his goblet earlier begin its work. The Emperor knew he would not be in this situation for long, and by the time he would accept the challenge as the existing champion, the Emperor would have succumbed to the poison.

Looking at the hilt of the Sword of Champions, the Emperor chuckled to himself. "This will be a very short battle. I am already weak," the Emperor thought as he waited for the challenge. "By accepting this farce, I will appear brave in the people's eyes. I will.

I know it with certainty," The Emperor thought as he recalled the secret pact he had made with the Chancellor many years ago. So far, he thought his strategy had worked.

First the demise of Valnass; then he'd set up the kidnapping of his whore of a wife, the Queen; last of all, the Emperor would take care of Montserrat himself.

"This has been in the making for a long time, and if the little brat hadn't left Darr, I would have been done with this a long time ago," he thought angrily to himself angrily.

The Emperor braced himself on the railing as a wave of nausea moved through his insides. "I won't let that spawn of my brother and his bitch rule this kingdom! I'd rather have the Darrn take over and destroy it!" The Emperor could not wait for the poison to finish its work, but he knew he must wait for the Darrn's challenge. However, the Chancellor was now drawing this event out too long. Growing more impatient, the Emperor felt hot and uncomfortable as the poison continued its purpose.

Now his restless thoughts began to transform into hatred. The Emperor out of revenge wanted the kingdom of Darr to suffer as much as he had.

"I have nothing more to lose! *Let* the people see what it is like groveling under the stench of the Darrn every day," the Emperor whispered evilly to himself as he looked at the Chancellor. "If the damn Trans would've been more efficient, I could've figured a way for this to have turned out differently."

With death drawing near, the Emperor's only regret now was that he wouldn't see his bastard nephew die by the hand of this filth. "I hate that boy!" the Emperor snarled angrily. He'd had enough of this sham, and as he drew the sword, he clanged it hard on his podium. The Chancellor realizing his opponent's impatience also saw he'd talked the Emperor into a lather.

Grabbing its own staff, the Chancellor with a loud voice proclaimed his Challenge: "By the rite of Supremacy and the conclusion of the Decade of Five, I, Chancellor Marsak, challenge you, the Emperor of Darr, to this fight for the Rite of Supremacy. Do you accept?"

As this challenge was called, a slew of Darrn warriors clawed themselves out from under the podium platform to form an attack pattern. Two of the younger beasts then quickly stationed themselves just below the Emperor's side of the podium. They took advantage of the absence of the Trans in this area and positioned their weapons for an attack.

The Emperor cleared his throat. But to his surprise, he was interrupted by another voice.

"I accept!" Montserrat said loudly. Then he stepped into the Emperor's and Chancellor's sight, next to the podium occupied by the Emperor. "Prince Montserrat, the Champion of the Mount, and rightful heir to the throne," he proclaimed.

Montserrat was stepping up onto the podium when the Emperor whirled around and yelled with hatred and gritted teeth, "You will never sit on the throne!"

The Emperor raised his sword and rushed to bring it down on the Prince. Suddenly, the poison began to take its full effect, and the Emperor buckled over in pain, and fell to the deck of the podium. Montserrat grabbed the twin-bladed sword, and easily pulled it from the Emperor's hand.

The prince looked at the dying man. Then he bent down and harshly whispered, "I know what you have done, my sister has told me everything. I would kill you now for my mother's death if you didn't deserve what you have coming to you."

Montserrat then picked up the crown, and placed it on his head. The surrounding Trans grabbed the fallen man and dragged him to the side of the podium. A Neptic shielded by a floating humidifier stuck a needle in the man's arm and administered the antidote. Montserrat stood by to see his orders followed; then he turned his attention on the arena.

16. THE FINAL BATTLE

Turning to the audience, Montserrat realized how much he had missed the overwhelming excitement that radiated from this arena. With a long breath and a reassuring hush that spread across the arena, Montserrat addressed the crowd.

"My fellow Darrians, I have come across a despicable conspiracy against our great and peaceful realm. One that has been brewing for years among the least suspected members of our house, and our most dangerous adversary, the Darrn. It has been a trying return from my exile because I have come back to deceit, civil rebellion, murder, and attempted treason from our beloved Emperor."

Unanimous gasps and murmurs were heard throughout the crowd as Montserrat paused from his announcement. "Attempted murder on myself and others has been followed out to keep me from being here today, as I was to be eradicated for one purpose: to seal everyone of this world into a life of slavery and torture from the Darrn. As we became victims of our predetermined fates, our dear Emperor would have taken his own life to escape our doom. Just before entering the arena, the Emperor administered the Stamis elixir to himself, and as a farce, *he* was to accept this challenge." Montserrat said while turning to his captor.

He looked at the pathetic leader with great repulsion yet also with a tender tug of memory for a man he once thought of as his father. Then Montserrat continued, "Sadly enough, we've paid for this travesty with our highest price: my mother and your most reverent Queen Aleon. With her lost to this evil plan of deception, I have taken the rightful position of defender for this Empire. I, Montserrat, am the Son of the rightful ruler of this throne, Valnass, the Emperor's older half brother and our Queen!" he proclaimed, raising his right hand.

In his grasp was his birthstone, and as he lifted the stone for all to see, it shone with such brilliance it was blinding. With this spectacle, there was no doubt the birthstone was the life force that identified the royal bloodline.

"The Trans restored their pledged allegiance to Darr as soon as they were aware of this situation, for as the truth was revealed, so was the truth and loyalty of the Imperial guard."

As Montserrat said this, the complete complement of Trans thundered to attention causing an eruption of noise as they readied themselves for any danger that may follow the Prince's next announcement.

"If I had not returned here to defend our throne, the Darrn were to rule for the next Decade of Five. If this was to evolve, we also would never have the ability to reclaim our rights again. Our Emperor has been at the head of this conspiracy with the Chancellor Marsak. I now offer our "Heroic" Emperor as a gift to the Darrn, and I accept this challenge for the last time." The victor's side will rule the kingdom forever—*winner takes all.* This will be the last Battle of Supremacy." Montserrat proclaimed. Using his levitating skills, he leapt high into the air off the podium and somersaulted to the ground in the arena.

Having the shining sword divide into the twin-battle blades, Montserrat landed between the two beasts; Montserrat swung upward with amazing speed, between the two young warriors standing on either side. The beasts looked at him with hunger, but it hit them suddenly that something was amiss. Confused, the Darrn stared down to see what was wrong; both warriors lost their balance as their upper torsos slid diagonally off of their remaining bodies. Montserrat looked at the next closest warrior approaching, and with his lash pistol, he blasted his attacker. It knocked the Darrn back. The beast growled as it spun around, and struggled to its feet, but the Prince was already upon him driving his blade through the spine of the animal. Montserrat twisted it twice, and slashed up to the heart of the beast while a gurgling sound burst out from the dying carcass. Montserrat dropped the hairy beast, and wiped its blood on his hand and arm onto his battle cape. Montserrat then leapt to the last warrior in the arena, and as he landed by the beast, it began swinging a bladed chain. The prince was generating an energy blast, as the Darrn roared with anger over the loss of the members of his clan. Keeping at a distance, the Prince watched as this Darrn warrior spun its octal-ended blades on one side of the chain and a barb studded mace on the other. The Prince then wrapped his cape around his left arm, and moved to a more defensive stance.

The Prince heard the shot, but it was too late to react. Just as Montserrat blasted this beast in front of him, with his energy ball, Montserrat was jerked back with such force it almost knocked him out. The Prince staggered for a bit, but quickly scrambled to his feet. The pain was excruciating as Montserrat saw the grappling hook sticking through his right chest close to the shoulder. Montserrat started to walk back to his fallen swords, but he was jerked back again by the clawed points of the hook, now piercing deeper into his chest. Montserrat looked back to see his assailant, but the chain pulling him was too taut for him to turn around or move closer to his weapons. The Prince darted backwards toward his attacker to give himself relief from some of the chain then whirled around as he heard another blast of hooks. When Montserrat spun away, the sound of metal clanked against the wall behind him. Montserrat saw the razor sharp chains as they lay slack next to the charred and oozing body of the Prince's last victim. The Prince turned to see his attacker and was in shock to see the size of this beast. It was the most hideous looking disfigured living animal Montserrat had ever seen. The attacking beast was a crazed and mutated Darrn with matted hair, and his filthy malodorous stench was wafting about in every direction of the arena. Now the odor was getting stronger as the beast was drew the Prince closer. The animal was drooling at his prize, and the fanged mouth was rabid as it growled a loud and long snarl.

Montserrat saw that his chances were slim as long as he was stuck to this chain unless he could quickly figure out a strategy. He grimaced as the pain shot through him again and the chain was tugged even harder. For a second time, the Prince ran back and turned to grab the slacked chain. He was grateful that his cape had not unraveled from his hand as the bladed chain cut into the cloth and into his hand from the weight.

While he pulled back, he ran toward the other chains on the ground. With his free arm, Montserrat used his scabbard to hook onto the other chains. Montserrat then ran around a giant pillar bracing them at the base. The beast pulled them back, and the chains dug into the solid stone, and stuck. The chains were not strong enough to cut through the pillar of marble, but the Prince now had a split second to react. As the Prince yelled from the pain, he brought his captor's chain down on the stuck chains and severed it just as the beast pulled on this chain hoping to reel Montserrat in for the kill. The remaining chain dangled from the Prince's back, and though it was heavy, he ran to his sword as fast as he could while the beast howled with disappointment from the loss of its prey. The Prince barely reached the sword before the hulking animal was upon him. He dodged it as a sweeping claw raked his back, latching onto the chain protruding from his shoulder and hurling the prince into a pile of oozing remains. The beast gave out a grumbling chuckle as the Prince's long sword stuck rigidly into the leg of the bronze statue of his father, Valnass, at the entrance to the Arena. The blade was shining in the artificial light flooding in from the stadium lights now that the moon had set.

Montserrat could see the weapon, but it was behind the beast and too hard for him to reach. The Prince frantically scrambled around for what he was looking for. As Montserrat felt the blood dripping from his own wound, he caught sight of the octal-chain lying under the remains of its dead owner. Gripping the chain, with all the energy he had left, he flung the heavy blades at the mutated beast now hovering over him. The beast blocked some of the blow to Montserrat's attack, but the chain wrapped around its muscular arm, and the blades all found a place in which they could embed themselves into the Darrn's tissue. Now with each contortion of its body, the animal growled in pain as the blades dug ever deeper. Seizing his only chance, Montserrat tossed the chain around the beast's head, and over his own sword to make a crude pulley. As he grabbed the mace, Montserrat tugged the ball digging the sharp spikes into his hands. Bracing himself around the foot of the statue, Montserrat pulled on the chain as hard as he could. The beast's weight anchored its body, and the awkward position of its arm around its head, caused the beast to drop its head down over the stuck sword. The sword sliced through the beast's exposed neck and decapitated him in one swift moment. The head fell with a sickening crunch as blood sprayed everywhere.

The crowd was now roaring with relief and victory, but knowing the battle was not yet won Montserrat climbed onto the Darrn's corpse and leapt to his sword yanking it from its resting place. Montserrat then looked around in a frenzy waiting for another attacker. That was when Montserrat spotted the Chancellor Marsak, and with a blaze of hatred in the Prince's eye, he flew to the podium. The Chancellor stepped back, and with a flash, raised its staff and shot two darts at the Prince. Montserrat raised his arm for protection, but the darts found their target. One dart hit his arm shackle and shattered. The other burrowed deep inside the Prince's forearm. Grunting, the Prince pounced like a beast and lunged at the Chancellor, pinning him down with his blade at the animal's throat.

"Enough! You lose!" the Prince growled as he leaned over the Chancellor.

The Chancellor began to laugh from his gurgling throat as it was grazed by the blade that was threatening its life.

"You are a fool, just as the Emperor has said! "You will not last long with that dart in your arm, and I made sure of that!" Marsak sneered as it pointed at the Prince's bleeding arm. "You may kill me, but you will die the same way I killed Valnass," the Chancellor growled so that only Montserrat would hear. Then it swallowed as the blade broke the skin, making it uncomfortable to speak. Montserrat now rose up and held his assailant down with the sword.

"That is where *you* are the fool, Chancellor, I have already taken the antidote to your poison," he explained pushing the tip of the blade down on the Chancellor. "We have all heard how honorable you are, but only a few know how devious you and your walking staff have become." At this last statement, the Master of the Guard stepped forward on the platform with help from his attendants.

"Hello brother," Minnion growled sarcastically as he approached the Chancellor. Marsak looked at his brother with wide astonishment. He couldn't believe that Minnion survived the torture he and his followers had inflicted on him.

"Why have you turned your back on us?" Marsak spit out as he now tried to escape his brother's approach. "You would rather be a slave to these people, and belittled for your heritage. I am disgusted with you. I would have received you back into the clan if you had come back to our side." It blurted out as it backed up into a wall.

"I would rather live in peace, and follow the path of the people who accepted me when I was cast out by you than to be an assassin of greater beings than you," Minnion retorted. Then he reached out with his clawed hand and ripped the clan's amulet from Marsak's neck. "I am the one that will make clan decisions now," Minnion snarled into Marsak's face. Minnion then turned, and walked away.

"You will not die here; I will send you to your own world with your puppet, the Emperor," the Prince proclaimed while dropping his blade. The Prince stepped away from the Chancellor. "You two can work things out while you are there in exile."

Nodding toward the guards, the Tran's swarmed in and took the Chancellor by force. The Prince looked at Minnion, and could see why his father Valnass was his best friend. Minnion bowed gingerly, and trailed behind the Trans to follow out the Prince's orders. As he turned, the Prince grabbed his shoulder, and said, "Thank you."

Minnion looked at him for a moment, and nodded. "Your father would be proud of you," he commented kindly, then left.

EPILOGUE

The next few months had been hectic since Montserrat was crowned Emperor of Darr in the Ceremony of Supremacy. His advisors helped him through the transition of power, and to his relief the people of Darr received him as their ruler. Montserrat never thought his uncle was a bad Emperor, but now to his surprise, there were many governing issues left unattended that now needed to be rectified. Montserrat looked down at his forearm and though his wounds had healed, the arm still irritated him slightly, so he rubbed it. The poisonous dart was still lodged in his arm's muscle, but its deadly effect had been stopped by the antidote Minnion had administered to him. It would always be there as a reminder of the treachery that had reached a climax during the battle of the Mount. Emperor Montserrat uncovered many conspiracies under his uncle's government, and he was astonished to realize that much of his uncle's vendettas and acts of treason had consumed his uncle like a malignancy. Montserrat knew that even if he could find all the traitors, there would always still be some form of rebellion. He would need to be alert and vigilant in his duties as ruler.

Montserrat had just received an information jewel, and was not surprised to hear Chancellor Marsak had been stripped of all its clan holdings on Darrn. The Darrn ruler had been forced into retirement from the government, and it was only permitted to live due to the fact it was once an arena warrior, though also the one to eliminate Montserrat's father, the Great Valnass. A few weeks after the conviction, Marsak was found dead—poisoned from a slow acting incurable agent. In reading this, Montserrat glanced at his battle sword and gave a brief smirk. His uncle had disappeared during his exile on the breeding planet Mugg. The last report received said he'd been tortured severely by Darrns upon his arrival but kept alive to suffer a slow painful sentence. Listening to the jewel, Montserrat wondered if he would ever see his uncle again or if this was that the end of it. Montserrat had just finished viewing these reports when Gojii walked into the room with her ladies-in-waiting.

Flowing fabric in gold and mauve fluttered around the women as they elegantly walked into his private chamber. The Emperor was mesmerized by his future Queen, remembering how his mother would catch the attention of everyone when she entered a room. The two lovers greeted each other, and Gojii took a seat near Montserrat as her attendants bowed and left the room quietly. Montserrat was pleased to see his woman, for Gojii had been very busy with the Lady Dreann on the affairs of the upcoming wedding. Gojii waited until the two were alone; then she got up and walked over to Montserrat. She put her graceful delicate arms around him and whispered in his ear and asked, "What would you like to do today my love?"

The Emperor smiled and took in the sweet aroma of her perfumed hair. He dropped the communication jewel as he stood, picked her up into his arms, and whispered back, "I feel like taking a bath."

ABOUT THE AUTHOR

Patrick S. Tremblay has written several short stories and children's books. He currently resides in Los Angeles, California with his wife and children and he is the co-founder of Rattledash Media, LLC.

www.ingramcontent.com/pod-product-compliance
Lightning Source LLC
Chambersburg PA
CBHW020730250626
47155CB00006B/2235